THE GRAYLING

BY

CHERYL FREIER

Written In Honor Of Martin Freier, My Husband: An Historical
Fiction Novel Based On Happenings During World War II

THE GRAYLING

Hidden Truths: Poems By Martin Freier

CHERYL FREIER

authorHOUSE®

AuthorHouse™
1663 Liberty Drive
Bloomington, IN 47403
www.authorhouse.com
Phone: 1-800-839-8640

Published by AuthorHouse   1/6/2011

ISBN: 978-1-4685-2407-9 (sc)
ISBN: 978-1-4685-2406-2 (hc)
ISBN: 978-1-4685-2405-5 (e)

Library of Congress Control Number: 2011962343

CONTENTS

Prologue

From the book: **HIDDEN TRUTHS, written** By: Martin Freier, who was himself a holocaust survivor. In the Prologue of this poetry book, Martin says, **MARTIN FREIER TELLS IT LIKE IT IS ....**

"Martin Freier is known in the Metro West Boston Area for his insightful columns and his radio broadcasts. In this book of poetry he tackles some very controversial subjects of life, death, and the Holocaust. (**I_ CON_X PUBLISHERS**) IBSN 0-9714528-0-6

Kristallnacht

On a night in November
in the middle of the night
the sound of glass
hit the pavement,
shattering it into pieces.
"Kill the Jews," they cried
as they broke the glass.
Above the echoes of the noise,
shrill greetings were heard
of "Heil Hitler" everywhere.
as innocent people died

that horrible night
many dreams were shattered
into little pieces.
That year
an early winter
followed November.,
Suddenly, the world became
much colder.

Over the years that followed
that night in November
was all but forgotten.
Only the wind
carefully carried
the pieces of glass
to each corner of the earth.
On each piece of glass
was a message from an
innocent soul.
The message was clear,
as clear as the morning light
that follows the moonlit night.
"Stop this hate,"
it said,
"before it's too late."

Though many have died,
no one paid heed
to the message carried
by the wind.
Somewhere in the mountains
covered with snow,
where no flowers grow,
the message was buried and
got lost.
No one knows at what cost.

So many years later
and lots of rain
failed to wash away the tears
and so much pain
of shattered pieces of glass
and many innocent dreams.

Mother At Eighty Eight

Though she's lost some of her zest,
for me she's still the best.
My mother's smile at eighty
eight
still lifts my spirit and faith.

Gone from her face and brow
is that former glow.
Yet, it feels so good for me to know
that this great lady is still there
and on her lips there's a prayer.

Whether she is happy or blue,
her love is so true.
Beneath her smile she hides
her pain.
Even on the days of rain
she sheds no tears
for all those bitter years
of suffering and travail.
Her lost loved ones she
remembers
in great detail.
They've been long gone,
murdered by the SS,
leaving no embers.
Their burned ashes
are scattered somewhere,
who knows where.
It's so unfair
we all declare,
though some wish to deny
without seeking to know why
young and old,
mother, father, sister, brother,
and child
were dragged out

in the middle of the night,
by those ready to commit
murder.
They were
never given a chance to fight to fight
for what's right.

Nothing's left of their remains,
not even a trace.
What a disgrace
for the whole human race!
But for her their memory will
always live on.

Say Kaddish

For the millions
of innocent souls
lost in the Holocaust
all we can do is offer
our Kaddish, the ancient prayer
or remembrance.

More than a prayer, it is our pledge to never forget
those who committed
the heinous crime,
a crime beyond reason,
beyond rhyme.
How quickly they spread the
hatred
that destroyed
everything that was sacred.
They set the flames,
wiped out countless names.

We ask the Lord to forgive
those who cared
but stood helplessly by
when they heard babies cry.

We pray for
those who dared
to sacrifice everything they
had.
They saved as many lives as
they could
to preserve the good.

Let us pray for
those who paid
the ultimate price
to put an end to this brutality
and to bring back

the sounds of liberty.

No tears can wipe away
those memories of yesterday.
No words we can say
can erase our horror, our
distress.
Those innocent lives, their loss
and the pain
will remain,
as we cry out never again.

And yet, we must be grateful to
the One Who
was there to do
what had to be done.
The Merciful One gave us
the faith to go on.
He dispersed the Hamans
and restored justice and law.
He gave us the courage to
rebuild on the ashes of
yesterday's sorrow
a new tomorrow.

A Speck Of Truth

The world is like a desert,
filled with sand,
Dust, smoke, and garbage
cover our beautiful land.
So many of us
scurry about in despair
and they fuss and fuss.
In this world of chaos
they're making it much harder
for us
to find someone we can trust,
though we know we must.
Truth is now buried beneath
the earth's deepest crust,
residing in a secret cave.
where only the brave dare to
seek truth's advice once or
twice.
Though truth's treasures
offer rare pleasures,
there for all to see,
our search for truth takes more
courage
than any of us can muster.
Instead, we give up and suffer
the sting of deceit,
Unexpected defeat.

Hope

Like a tiny beam of light,
hope streams through a crack
through the tiniest pores of the
human body.
Up the blood stream
it flows through the veins
with renewed vigor,
until it reaches the heart
and our brains.
The tiny beams of hope
wreak havoc with our
imagination
that lies dormant
and helpless in hibernation.
It sets our imagination
on fire until
without explanation, pellets of
joy
and happiness spurt forth
to all our senses,
making us forget all our past
tenses.

In a world that was once sad
and filled with emptiness,
our senses
spring to life and make us feel
glad
we're alive
as we begin to see
life's beauty
and the possibilities for our
greatness.

Chapter I

Acceptance Of The War

Moments in time remain with us in our memories until our death. These moments are our own personal chronicle of history; and sometimes it is a happy history; and sometimes it is the story of tragedy. War with its hatreds, bitterness, fighting, starvation, bombing, fires, mechanisms of destructions and death came to our country, Czechoslovakia in the year, 1939. Moments in time changed for everyone in the world.

People in the world were shocked over the war's beginning, but the impact of the real exigencies of the war had not penetrated people's consciousness—for they were human and had a muted sense of reality. After all, who knew that this war was a war designed to conquer and to control the world and to be the war of all wars. The machinery of war moved quickly, capturing, evading, and prodding forward with the sound of tanks and guns, bombs, and the roar of airplanes prowling the clouds in the skies over Europe. There are those who would deny it ever happened. For those of us who were there and were hunted like animals, there is always the feeling of loss and sadness when remembering all that one experienced.

Every year since the Germans took over the country, no one could be the same. Adrenalin levels never rested. It was an instant defeat for our peaceful way of life--praying at our Temples, going to work and making a living, and for us young ones, studying in school. It affected the food that we ate, and the clothes that we wore. It affected the air that we breathed. It affected our freedom. It affected our ability to dream that life would improve for us.

As the war raged, and we marked the months of occupation on the calendar, and with an indelible marker in our minds; the longer the war went on, the worse it got—the more fierce the fighting. We knew that sooner or later the fighting would come to our town, Micholovce.

In the beginning we went about our daily business, but as the days passed my father heard one story after another about people disappearing; at first it was the businessmen who traveled from city to city who never returned. The feeling of helplessness overtook us all, but our abiding love for our God sustained us and reignited a spirit of hope somehow within us. We prayed in our homes and the prayer for sustaining life became more real day after day. We began to realize that this war was not going to go away. Many of us consulted the Rabbi of our large congregation and magnificent synagogue. He told us to stay. Every time we questioned him, this was his answer.

For the Sabbath and for the Jewish holidays, the men gathered in basements where they knew they were not followed; they said the prayers but their minds were thinking about the Germans at the same time. The prayers helped us to overcome our fears of dying and were an excellent means of defying the Germans, and this sustained us. Many people planned to conserve food and planned hiding places in order to escape from the Nazis. An extra room behind the closets was the going thing to work on. Digging tunnels from basements was another plan devised by many. Food was hoarded and buried for the day when there would be no food. Every day that we survived was a triumph. Every day was a new way of life, which was so different from our peaceful and spiritual existence.

I was certain that the animal soul within us would surface, but this was a time when we needed the combination of the spiritual life and the animal soul. Our whole routine changed. My mother no longer watched us as we left for school. We slept long hours in our beds, so that the days would be shorter. My grandfather Jacob lived with us and he always knew a nice way to say to us children, "Quiet down now". He would always say to me, especially, "Come over and sit with me, and I will read you a story". It would always be a story from the Bible and then we would talk about the characters in the story. Then he would fall asleep in his chair, and I would sit by his side watching him, while finishing the book.

In the beginning, the movement against the Jews in Micholovce was subtle. Lists were secretly compiled of the names of the Jews. The list made no distinction to man, woman, or child. Even a newborn Jew was considered an enemy of the state. Everything was subtle, but people who were taken away from the ghetto never returned. They seemed to have disappeared. But by chance one or two men escaped from their rapacious captors and returned to tell the truth about what was happening.

People were shattered, shaking with fear, as they heard the ominous truth about the devil, named Hitler, and his bunch of barbarians, and their master plan to eradicate all of the Jews. Jews were being rounded up and forced to remove their clothing. They were forced to stand naked in front of deeply dug pits. With wild, shattering bullets released against them, they fell to their deaths. The soft sound of a final breath reverberating could still be heard despite the loud sound of the thunderous rifles. The very few who woke up and managed to climb through the mangled, bloody, gray-colored, rigid, cold bodies, were never able to forget the horrors of this experience.

Trembling, fear, agony, crying, the sound of wailing grief could be heard from each home in the ghetto. Some people gave up and succumbed in their own beds. Others built secret cellars. Yet, others built rooms behind secret walls. Some built tunnels. A few packed up their belongings and gave themselves a chance to make their own fate, by trying to escape. Others planned carefully, strategizing how to board a boat with an attempt to escape to the land of Israel. Some were able to purchase false identification papers and were able to cross the border of their country, beginning a new life in another city far away from their homes, and families, and businesses, and temples.

Joseph's older brother, Samuel, approached him about money from his share of the lumber business. Joseph promised to come up with the cash to buy him out. Joseph sold what he could: a valuable diamond necklace, an heirloom pearl necklace, and took cash from a business vault.

Sam left the country with his wife and daughter with a guide as soon as he had the money. He traveled first to Casablanca, and then when he could arrange safe passage to the United States, he arranged passage on an ocean liner for the United States. He made it. He was very lucky.

Chapter 2:

Joseph's Plan To Escape

Joseph Freier decided to take his family across the border and to board a train to Switzerland. He contacted friends and family whom he knew he could trust and he asked if anyone knew a guide who could be trusted. One day, three weeks later, a friend knocked softly on his door. Joseph opened the door quickly and with both eyes peering at one time in every direction around his house, he let the friend in. He closed the door with a quick thrust and excused himself for his abruptness. He stood straight with the inside of the door arching his back, all 5'8" of him. He moved his right arm forward and pointed his finger towards the kitchen, and he pushed his glasses closer to his eyes.

His friend sat straight with his feet firmly touching the polished wooden floor. "You must leave tonight", he said in a most assured tone of voice. Joseph closed his eyes for a second and then nodded his head as if to say, "Okay, I will do it". He stammered and cleared his voice and asked, "Can you help us to escape?" His friend, whom Joseph had known since boyhood and who for many years had invited Joseph for a family lunch, after he came home from Christian church services on Sundays. Joseph looked carefully into his friend's eyes, and he knew to trust him, and said, "Okay, we will go".

Joseph ran up all 14 stairs in one minute, calling the names of his four sons and one daughter----all in one breath. Anna, his wife, heard him, walked in from the garden and asked, "What is the commotion?" Joseph quipped with an air of determination, and said, "we're leaving and that is all there is to it".

A few hours later, they all sat quietly at the kitchen table, and they waited, as the night got darker and darker. When it was pitch-black outside, they got up, and they knew that it was follow the leader and that the leader was Joseph. Standing tall with an undying faith and determination, they walked out quietly onto the road. They felt free. The winds from the night air wind blew onto their faces. They could not hear a sound, and the silence was golden. They smiled in relief. They could barely see their guide in front of them. My father led the way. He had taught himself to chirp like a bird so that he could signal us for danger. We were all on the alert for the sound of the bird call. The woods grew closer as the darkness from the trees created a blinking blindness of its own kind—the black grew darker and darker. I remember us stopping once. My father thought that he had heard a noise. My father whispered to us that we should start crawling into the woods from this point. We got down on our hands and feet and crawled. The ground was soggy and the soil glued our hands so we had to stop to stand up and brush off the dirt. The ground looked ugly; it looked like leaves had decayed, untouched, for all the ages. Our arched backs ached. Our eyes, which were bulging from the strain of seeing the heels of our shoe in front of us, ached and tingled. I remember crawling for miles. I remember oozing into the softness of the earth and feeling uncannily shielded by the black earth and trees. Our breathing got belabored and when my mother called out, with her hands shaking through her thick gray strands of hair, "oh, help, I cannot go any farther, we all collapsed and lay for hours on the damp and cold ground. As it was the month of August, the soil was somewhat softer and this made it easier for us to move along the winding roots in and around the large, black and sturdy tree trunks, which we used as our pathway. The trees had grown in this forest for hundreds and hundreds of years.

The nighttime darkness was relentless. They walked slowly amongst the tall, thick, dependable statues of the trees, feeling their way, often touching the outside bark of the trees; the trees seemed everlasting and nourishing to the soul. The trees were a force of power that Martin admired. The trees had grown in this forest for hundreds and hundreds of years.

Owls perched on the high branches, occasionally leaving out a hooting sound that reverberated through the airwaves of the wind and wisely warning the family, saying, "Whoever comes this way, beware". Joseph became unnerved by the sound of the owl, and whispered in Martin's ear, "maybe the owl knows something that we don't know". Martin focused his eyes more on the sides of the pathways.

The sun's light for the next day was beginning to appear, and the sun shined brightly through the small spaces in-between the green leaves. The waving, light green, yellow-speckled, iridescent, tall, pointed leaves were extensions of the branches at the apex arches of the trees. Soon the darkness from the night would disappear like puff into the air; the new day would bring light and hope for the oppressed.

Their guide motioned with his uplifted left hand for them to stop. He held his hand steady; the family looking sleepy, but they all stopped quickly. The weight of their bodies made footprints in the soil, burrowing lasting, irrevocable imprint marks of the date and times in the forest floor. Their story of their quest to survive was recognized by the animals and the creatures in the forest and was recorded by time itself. Animals, grey wolves, pine martens watched them from behind the trees.

The guide motioned with his left hand that they all squat behind the bushes, and he squatted down. Following his example, they dropped the small amount of baggage that they had and they squatted down as far as they could go. Joseph motioned to his son, Henry, the youngest understood; he knew at a young age of five that there was no time for crying. The muscles in their arms and legs ached. The muscles numbed. Their eyes stared out into space. Fleeting moments heard the rapid beats of hearts' racing. Sweat appeared on all of their brows even though the weather had become much colder. The new month had just started but the moment in time was an eternity.

The guide stood up and motioned with his right hand, pressing on his pursed lips. Everyone knew to be quiet. They knew to listen. Martin's thoughts wandered to the Jewish people's escape from Egypt. "The ruler of Germany had become like the pharaoh and his princes", he said silently to himself He muttered to himself, "history is reliving itself, and we, the Jews in Czechoslovakia are the slaves of this generation". He closed his eyes, and he said to himself, "may God deliver us from this evil".

The minutes went by as though time would never again move. Martin transfixed his thoughts on Moses leading his people, the journey through the dessert. He pictured Moses in his mind with a striped, multi-colored robe, which was made out of lamb's wool. He asked himself the question, "Were not the forces of evil more prevalent in the desert?" and then he thought, "Oh, yes, they were". Then he thought, "But then the people traveled behind the ark with the covenants". He lifted his head and closed his eyes tightly until they ached and then he thought, "When God wishes to provide an ark for his chosen people, then he will".

Martin felt an inner spirit moving from within him to the outside.

There was a thin yellow glow for a moment's time that covered his body. He was not able to speak at that moment. He felt warmth returning to the inside of his body; it was almost as though he felt a sense of warmth after having eaten a satisfying meal on the Shabbat. He found himself looking up at the bright full moon in the sky. He had a smile on his face.

His silent thoughts were interrupted as he thought he saw the guide getting up. He was mistaken. The guide was just shaking his leg. "Yes, Martin said to himself, "wherever the ark went, it destroyed the forces of evil and then the people could enter safely into the promised-land".

his eyes, and he said to himself, "may God deliver us from this evil".

The guide was getting up slowly, and it looked as if he was watching something!! No longer were there thoughts of the Sabbath---those thoughts were a distance of happiness away in time", Martin thought. He recited, "Hear O' Israel", and he felt his breathing less labored, but he clasped both fists.

Motions were spotted in the distance—shadows mingling with the trees. Sounds were heard: the hooting of the owls' watchful eyes, the sound of the wind's swooshing, and the crisp, crackling sound of the fallen leaves being stepped on by the on-comers. Footsteps could be heard, but not the usual rhythm of the Nazi boots, so Joseph breathed steadier, and his children did not cringe with fear.

A second guide appeared suddenly about six yards away, as the condensation of new dew rising from the ground slowed their pace. The second guide was followed by a family, four people; they looked tired, bedraggled, and were dragging their feet. The couple's sons looked like they were older, may 15 and 17. The family and the second guide stopped a few yards away from the bushes, which Joseph's family was hiding in.

They stood looking around........They waited. They sat down on the forest floor, easily adjusting to the coldness of the ground and the bumps and crevices and unevenness of the surface of the ground, as the winds picked up a bit and swooshed around them. It seemed like an hour had gone by, but it was hard to tell time. No one moved. Joseph's guide did not give the signal for Joseph and his family to join the second guide.

Then the second guide said "I do not like it. We were supposed to meet with two other groups. Let us take a chance and make a run for it". They quickly followed the stance of the guide, and they began to run towards the way that would bring them to the train, but they knew that they were to travel south through the wooded areas to Bratislava and then they were to depart on a train in Austria for Switzerland.

The family of four faded into shadows among the trees. Martin felt like reaching out to them and calling them back. Martin wanted to say to the boys, "I am coming too, and maybe we can study together someday, or join a team of soccer players?" He knew that he could not. Joseph was thinking, "I think I know this family". He is a jeweler in another town". Anna was thinking, "The woman looks like she is my age". The winds whistled around Joseph and his family; and they, who tempted the swirls of the winds to go around them, Anna and Joseph, knew not to speak.

Then suddenly, popping loudly, destroying the sweet sound of silence and the emergence of a new day; scooping up the waters of the dew with their boots, were tall soldiers. They looked like disfigured shadows, as they marched through the spaces between the trees; they were clad in woolen uniforms; and through the weary, tired eyes of the pursued, the soldiers looked like they were colored red; they were a virtual lineup of clones; they were all shouting in a frenzy, echoes of voices seemed to come from deep within the earth.

The wicked sound of dogs pursuing their prey erupted into another frenzy of loud sounds, a halyard of barks to rig their victims. Bright lights, blinding lights, which were grasped tightly by the clones, shined their ominous rays of fate on the family of four and their guide. The guide tried to flee to the shelter of nearby trees, but the speed of one of the soldier's piercing bullets stopped him in his tracks. He fell in a moment. More shots were heard. The rustling sound of falling leaves was heard afterwards. Then silence, as the trees in the forest noted what had happened and the branches shuddered.

Terror struck through the pumping ventricles of Joseph Freier's heart. He recited a prayer, "Hear oh, Israel", silently and waited in the exact spot that he stood and he did not move a muscle. Joseph's family followed suit by closing their eyes and waiting. Martin looked up to the heavens through a clearing of an extended arm of trees, and said to himself, "they have all gone to God and they are living in the land of Adam and Eve, with plenty all around them and no fears. He visualized one of the sons dancing with a fiddle in his hand and the other son dancing and ringing the bells of a tambourine. He visualized the mother and father holding hands, while they climbed the steps to heaven. They looked healthy and not bedraggled. Their bodies lay still, however. The watching trees refused to absorb the blood of innocent Jews into their root system.

A voice boldly shouted, "Dead Jews, just leave them here to rot", and the formation of vicious clones formed a line and vanished slowly into the air. They passed through the other side of the dark curtain of death, which descended into the earth a long way down. Joseph and his family stayed in the woods until Joseph's guide stood up and raised his hand, pointing his hand in the direction of their town. With hopes diminished for escape, they trudged home, never muttering a word. Martin prayed silently for deliverance.

CHAPTER 3:

INFORMATION ON US AS A FAMILY

Even though we were children, we understood that there was a dangerous war raging, but we did not have the maturity to go beyond those thoughts, and this sense of 'denial' was a blessing for us. My brother Sam was the oldest. Sam was only 14 in 1944, but the lines on his forehead and his red, ruddy complexion were a clear indication that he had seen cruel things that no man should see. He looked a lot older than he was for he was tall for his age and had a very stoic expression on his face. With blond hair and steel blue eyes, he looked like the Germans. He could speak German fluently and other languages too.

Joseph, our dad, as a young boy had attended schools in Germany; he had lived in Germany with an aunt; he spoke the language fluently and he taught the boys the language. They caught onto the language very quickly.

Myself, Martin, I was 3 years younger than Sam. I was big for my age, standing tall and lanky, while Sam was tall and broad. A question was always on the expression of my face; so I looked as though I might be 15; at 15 a lot was expected of a young man: to study; he had to choose a vocation, and to think about a bride----a wife and family for his future. I realized that with the war the whole course of my life had completely changed. But I knew not to cry. I knew to act as though I was 11 years old, which if I survived, I would be soon anyway.

My mother had come from an 'aristocratic background'. Her father, I will always remember him----he drove the carriage with the two horses in the front, calling out, "Hudya, hudya", and I had to hold onto my hat and hold tight onto my seat or I would lose both. My grandpa Hellinger was a soda maker and the only one in the whole town. He manufactured the soda and delivered the soda to the people all over the ghetto and also outside of the ghetto. His business got bigger and bigger each year.

In the beginning of the war, we could forget about the dangers and continue with the business. As the days passed, more and more restrictions were placed on us. But still, we were in denial and hoping that the war would end soon. We always hoped that our way of life would resume soon.

We hoped that we could forget about impending bombs; we hoped that we could forget about the throes of hunger. My father was not happy that, "we should forget about the war for he knew that forgetting would undermine our chances for surviving. My father wanted us to be prepared. He asked us "Who amongst you would want to be the 'watchman' for planes"? We looked at my father with staring eyes; our mouths mumbling with fears at the thought of planes swooping over our rooftops and aiming bombs over our town and our people.

"Okay, then I will choose," and he chose my younger brother Henry. He told him, "I have chosen you, because you run so quickly, and no one, not even the German soldiers would think that someone your age would be the watchman. He said, "You Henry are like the tribe leader, Naphtali...... you run faster and fleeter than the fastest deer. You will do a fine job". He walked with Henry and explained, "You see that hill up there before the woods, well, each day I want you to climb up the hill and watch for the motorcycles and the planes". He paused. "Your sister Edith will bring you food to eat and will stay with you for a little while". He smiled and looked at Henry and asked politely, "Do you understand?" Henry nodded his head.

One day went by. Two days passed by, and then a month, and then months; we were spared some of the initial strategic verve of conquering, because we lived near the Russian border and the Germans were not entrenched in the outskirts of our town yet. We waited for Henry to tell us that the Germans were coming every day. All of our neighbors for blocks and blocks were waiting to find out too. Henry felt he was doing something so important that he grew to be less frightened.

The war continued to wage. It became common to see the lights of the cannons and the guns in the night time even though they were many miles away. People who had escaped from these towns had stories of terror to tell about the Germans. They talked of round-ups of people, they talked of deportation trains, and they talked of long marches.

CHAPTER 4

THEN THE GERMANS CAME

Then one day Henry saw a lot of dust of clouds on the ground, moving like the wind and he knew. We were speared nearly one year. What Henry spotted was two motorcycles coming towards our town. He ran down the hill, one foot running forward and then the other running even faster---just like wheels with spokes—his feet turning and turning. His arms almost extended straight out from his sides---he for these moments was an airplane; his voice being without a natural ring, but this time his voice had the ring, as he called out like a bell, "The Germans are coming, the Germans are coming. Doors slammed, women screamed, men shouted, windows banged down hard. This was the music of horror.

We sat frozen in time. Visions of prisoners being marched before the triumphant Germans wearied our brows and the pits of our stomachs. In no time at all, echoes bounced from house to house, ceiling to ceiling. The word was out in whatever language you spoke that the Germans were coming! We heard the sound of the motorcycles coming. It was a coarse sound as if blazing against time and pushing the innocent angels away. They came closer and closer. The two descendants from the Amalachites, the German soldiers delivered the message, "We will be taking over the town", they yelled this message as loud as they could in a course, guttural, hoarse sounding voice. It meant death to most, fear to most, thoughts of escape were on everyone's mind. The message was clear and we knew that at the very least we would be part of a round-up. From there, we did not know. As they thumped on their gas pedals, we heard the engines roaring like wild panthers and they disappeared quickly into the blackness of the night. Only their sound could be heard in the distance and the memory of their passing through was indelible.

We wondered what to do about the Sabbath, which was the next day, but our question was soon answered as we heard the rolling of the thick rubber tires pouncing on the small cobblestones beneath them. Shattering sounds to the ears---grinding, irking, pulling, prodding, pushing--- sounding all at one time; something like the wild panther jumping for the kill of his prey-------we could hear others being taken into their chilling machine.

Very few of us could escape, especially with the responsibility of caring for children. The loud noises of the motors of their trucks, the constant grinding and the shouting of the soldiers, the loudness, as the butts of their rifles knocked harshly on the doors of our neighbors drowned out all other sounds in our ears. No natural sound could be heard. No sound of a robin chirping. Then the sound of quick-paced, heavy steps came closer to our front door, while we sat spellbound on the kitchen chairs. Quiet. A moment of reprieve…. Loudness….. Worse loudness…… Fierce loudness……. As the sound of the rifle butt was beating at the door, my father, Joseph, got up from his chair. He stood on the other side of the door and waited. When the door was almost busted down, he opened the door, and pretended that he had just gotten up from a deep sleep.

Three soldiers walked right in as though they owned the place. Imprints of their footprints with mud as a medium stained the cleaned, swept kitchen wooden floor. Spots of the mud will always remain. Damn spots. "Come", they shouted, and they pushed us to the door. We were led. We were led like sheep. This was my biggest regret, allowing myself to be led like a sheep. I remember feeling the cold from the weather biting on my skin. This was an outward sensation. Inwardly, I felt like a coward.

We were piled into the back of the truck, seeing the dark eyes in the background, was the first thing that we saw. They were the frightened faces of close cousins and friends and neighbors. My feet felt numb, and feeling like reaching for a floor when there was no floor. They closed the truck door, and I heard the click of the lock, and the truck started on its way--- -my thoughts then were---- what if the Jews were the conquerors and the Germans were the vanquished, would we do the same?

What saved us from complete despair was that we were together. We prayed silently, while we knew that we were praying the same prayers. Not a single person spoke. A woman sobbed and wiped her nose in a handkerchief. Another woman was holding a young baby and patting the baby on the back to quiet it; and it worked for a little while, but the baby was hungry and there was no food. She put her finger in the baby's mouth, and he sucked on her finger. But it was not food, and everyone knew that the baby would soon cry again.

An old man was bending his knees as though he needed to sit. Finally he fell down, but he seemed to be more comfortable, even though his legs jotted out and twisted in-between the legs of other men. We rode over bumpy roads. All of us listened most intently for turns and stops, trying to figure out where we were going. We had become spies for ourselves---watching, looking, seeking, searching, and in our hearts----running away from the terror----in our minds, however, it was our imaginations that saved us, because there was always that one percent of all of us that could not believe that this was happening!

And then, just when our patience was exhausted and the agony of our discontent and fears began to surface, the truck stopped. Not that my fears were allayed, but I thought that we would be able to breathe in fresh air, and I was right---at least that way I felt that we were treated more like humans and not like cattle.

The back doors were opened with the sound of a jerk and then a big pull. And in the same moment of almost lost consciousness from lack of air, we were told to get out. As we jumped off the back of the truck, a moist mist sprinkled upon us from above. We looked up and saw that it was coming from a very large cloud.

We were told to follow the soldier who was in front of us. We followed one lone guard. We marched single file along a winding dirt trail, and came to a large fenced in area, which looked just like a pen. We were told to go in. Hundreds of people were already there. The fence was a mesh wire, a thin mesh wire, a flimsy wire I was thinking. Sam and my father were thinking the same thing. One lone guard walked up and down the front of the pen. He carried a rifle on his shoulder.

Sam, my older brother, who had the same height and coloring as the German soldiers made believe he was blowing on his hands and motioned to my father that he was going to the back of the pen. Joseph understood. Sam pushed his way politely past the people and quickly lifted the wire and crawled underneath and disappeared into the nearby woods. My father followed him. Then I followed. Then my brothers went under the fence quickly like two snakes, and then my mother and my sister went under the fence together. My mother always had to hold my sister's hand. My mother's eyes were watery, but she knew she had a chance to escape, and she soon joined us in the woods. I was proud of Sam. I was proud of myself. We had done a good evading the Nazis. We had escaped. We had escaped quickly. No one complained on us either. Others must have followed us after we had gone.

CHAPTER 5

GETTING OUR NAMES OFF OF THE GERMANS LIST

We had prepared, but as Joseph commented just as he felt we were safe from any German pursuers, we had taken too big a chance. Joseph suggested that we use strategy. Joseph suggested that the next time that the Germans came that he would go and escape through the attic. That way he could come later to rescue us. All agreed. In the meantime, Joseph said, "I must tell my foreman to take our names off of today's roundup list. We slept in the woods that night. We were hungry, but a safe place to sleep was our concern.

Joseph reached the house of his friend and foreman and wiping off the sweat from his brow, and a little dizzy from the long walk and not having eaten for at least eight hours, he knocked on the window pane of the living room. "Hurry up", he muttered to himself, and breathed a sigh of relief as he saw a figure from the back of the room coming forward and he could make out the features.

The figure came closer and closer until he stopped and looked out the window, looking sharply in every direction as he deftly placed his hands under the bottom of the window and yanked the window up. He motioned with his left hand out of habit and said softly, "come quickly", and Joseph very quickly put his head through the window and placed his hands evenly on the bottom sill and heaved himself up. He landed with the bottom of the soles of his shoes firmly pressing against the ground and he sprang forward. "Please", he beckoned in a pleading voice, "help me and my family".

Frank nodded his head up and down and then with the furrows of the brows becoming more pronounced, he said, "I know the assistant to the mayor of the town." You must stay here in this room. Danielle will bring you food. You must not leave until I get back, and he looked at Joseph with a very serious expression on his face. Joseph replied, "I will listen to you. But when will you be back?" Frank asked, "Is there an emergency?" Joseph replied, "Yes. I left Anna and the children in the woods". Frank paused, with the left index finger under his chin, and said, "I shall be back in two hours." Joseph nodded his head up and down, sighed by blowing some air out of his mouth, and smiled. He sat down in the large green velvet chair and waited.

Frank shut the front door quickly as he ran down the stairs. He passed many houses on the street. He passed two Nazi soldiers, but they did not stop him. They were talking and smiling as they walked along the sidewalk. Frank turned quickly into a side street and walked a few paces and came to a house on the top of the hill that was surrounded by fresh green fertile grasses. He walked up the brick laden walk and before knocking on the door, he swiftly turned his head and looked around to see if anyone was there.

He knocked on the door twice and a little, elderly, frail-looking lady opened the door a few inches and peered through the opening, while saying, "What can I do for you Frank?" Frank quickly interjected, "I must speak to Bernard immediately," and he had a stare coming out of both gray-green colored eyes. The woman opened up the door and said, "very well, come in please, and quickly", and she closed the front door very swiftly. Frank ascended the light blue carpeted spiral stairway. No time for even taking a few breaths after he reached the top step, he darted down the wide hallway, passed three bedrooms, and reached the fourth bedroom, which served as a library, in the matter of a few minutes.

He knocked gently on the door and a voice quickly answered, "Come in, please", and nodded his approval by waving his right hand two times. Bernard said, "what brings you here so early in the morning?" Frank said, "Joseph Freier has escaped from the Germans and would like to have your approval. Bernard bit hard on the thick and well-buttered toast he was eating and said, "three hundred dollars and his name will be off of the German list". "But", Frank stammered, "what about Anna and the children?" "Oh, I will throw them into the bargain", and he bit harder into the piece of toast and reached for a hard boiled egg. Frank stammered, "I will bring you the money". Bernard waved his left hand towards the door and said, "Then it is done". Frank descended the stairway quickly, jumping over the last three steps. He saw the lady standing by the door and he said as he held the brow of his brown cap, "thank you very much", and he departed, becoming quickly a dot in the horizon.

He walked quickly at a hurried pace, careful to look ahead and behind himself, though every few minutes. He unlocked the strong wooden front door to the house and Joseph could hear the thick footsteps as the leather soles of Frank's shoes stepped firmly on the cushioned rug. Frank said, "It is all set for $300.00."

And he paused, "you do have the money", he said in a polite tone of voice. Joseph did not hesitate so he came forth and said, "I have the money at my house". Frank said, "Fine then". And he paused and shaking a bit, he said, "We shall go together just as soon as it is really dark out". Joseph nodded and pondered for a while for the best way to go with the least problem of detection by the Germans or any of their spies. He then said to Frank, "I think that the best way to go is by car" And he paused for a moment and then asked with a questioning tone of voice, "Do you have petrol?" Frank said, "Don't worry about it! We will make it to your house and back easy". It was really dark out and it was after 8 o'clock and with a hot thermos in his hands and some freshly baked bread, he said, "Joseph, open up your side", and they left with a sputter of smoke from the exhaust and a yanking, cranking sound of the clutch.

They rode on the back roads and wherever there was light and when he was able to see the road, Frank dimmed the lights. They had ridden for fifteen minutes when Frank said, as he cleared his voice, "It may be too far to the Jewish quarters". They rode for another 20 minutes along the hills and curves, the car reacting with an occasional sputter, and gaping noise as the car descended into a hole in the road and then by its own force, pushed itself out. "Aha, I see the house on top of the hill", Joseph shouted and he smiled, thinking, at least there is a home to go back to".

As they got out of the car, Joseph shouted, "come with me to the back yard", and with a slight grunt and a look of questioning, Frank followed. "You see that big tree over there?" Joseph said, and he pointed to it, as Frank wiped his eyes with a handkerchief and nodded his head, as he said, "yes". "I will walk five feet from the branch that is hanging down, and then I will dig for the money".

Frank rubbed his brow, and watched carefully. Joseph counted as he walked the five feet and then cropping down on the ground, he started to dig with his hands. "Here", Frank said, "as he struggled to pull off his jacket with both hands at the same time, "I will help you", and he cropped down and started grabbing the earth and then throwing it over his shoulder. Joseph felt a tin box and said to Frank, "We shall have the money in a minute". Lifting up the tin box, he winced as he said, "I am hoping that we will all survive this war". Frank nodded, but then noticed a second box underneath. What may I ask is this second box for? The second box contains the family's Bibles. And the tin box which is below that one contains the family's jewels which have been handed down for generations.

They were in the car a few minutes later. Frank loaded up with $300.00 cash and Joseph took $200.00 for himself. When they came near a bend in the road, Joseph pointed as he said to Frank, "Do you see that clearing where the trees have been cut down?" Frank squinted and then focused and then said, "Yes, I see it". "Well, let me off there". Frank put his feet on the clutch, and on the brake, and stopped the car, and placed the shift in the correct slot, and then released his left foot from the clutch, and his right foot from the brake, feeling a gnawing sensation that pulsated every once in a while in the middle of his knee cap.

Joseph left the car quickly and Frank put the car into gear and the car darted, inched back, jerked and then propelled forward. Joseph bent his head and held his hands in the front of his face as he walked slowly and carefully to the clearing where he had left Anna and the children. "Not too far", he said to himself, "have been in these parts so many times looking for lumber", and he paused as he reminisced, "so many times I took a crew into these woods and we chopped down the logs and hauled them away" He shook his head out of disbelief as he muttered, "I never thought I would find it handy in escaping from the Germans". He shook his head several times. He stopped once or twice and looked up, while he was making his way through the thick, and tall, and untouched multitude of the cluster of trees.

His mind veered, thinking about the Sabbath and how Anna took all day to prepare for the Sabbath. She cleaned the house, dusting and sweeping for most the morning. In the afternoon, she collected her apples, and walnuts, and raisins; and remembering all of the ingredients by heart, she rolled out the dough for the strudel and then put in the chopped apples, and walnuts, and raisins, remembering to roll the dough with its precious contents several times over. The strudel was finished always within the hour and everyone ate to their heart's content. There was always a full table of food for the Sabbath.

Anna grated all of the potatoes and a few big onions and mixed the mixture with a little bit of flour and two eggs and then in one hour, behold, the whole house smelled of cooked potato pudding. Who could resist eating this fine baked food?" There was rice pudding occasionally and there were always at least two well baked chickens, which were bought special from the kosher butcher. There was always the delicious chicken soup, which warmed our hearts and our souls in the winter time and also in the hot weather—all year round soup---to slurp up quietly and roll your eyes from side to side as you look at everyone else at the dinner table, and blow hard at the smoke coming from the soup on your tablespoon.

The aroma of the barley and the corn and other vegetables all melded together to make you sense the sweetness of the good food. It was satisfying to say the least. The stoves were kept heated all night, provided warmth, particularly, on very cold winter nights. The melding of the large brown beans with the long, peeled potatoes with eggs, left to cook in their shells was more than satisfying. Ah, but to sit at the Friday night meal at the Sabbath and at the luncheon after morning services", and he repeated the words, "the Sabbath over and over again". Tears started to flow and he had to stop where he was in the middle of the woods and headed to a destination where he left his wife and his children. He had trouble stopping these overwhelming thoughts. He cried out, "why?" and fell to his knees prostrate to the ground. He remained in this stupor for what seemed like an eternity and cried.

A bird flew over him and landed on a tree branch that was above him. The bird chirped sweetly and softly and moved its head from left to right. Like a bell startling a person who is contemplating deeply, the bird startled Joseph and as he wiped his eyes with his clean, white linen handkerchief and he blew hard as his lips stretched and moved forward. He had faced death and bad times before, but he said to himself, "never like this".

A voice shot out of the wilderness as though one of the trees were talking. A young male's voice called out with a strong sense of authority, "who goes there?" And Joseph smiled as a cracking noise from one of the bramble brushes gave way and tore under his left boot. Joseph called out loudly with his chin up, "it is your father, Sam". And like lightning a figure darted out from behind the huge trunk of the tree that was about three yards in front of Joseph. In the middle of the silence of the woods, two men ran to each other and hugged each other tight, clinging to express the miracle of being alive and being well in a war that promised to kill all of the Jews.

"Father, you must be tired and hungry. Let me help you", and Joseph, a man of 45 yielded and the son held his father's arm tightly and they walked towards the clearing. They soon saw Anna and the children. The boys had devised a game just like hopscotch and with a stick Martin was etching out the numbers to put into each square. Martin was jumping from square to square as the other boys looked on and cheered. Edith was holding a doll, which Bernard had managed to whittle out of a large tree branch. Anna was mixing berries and mushroom in a hold in the ground. Anna waved and looked up to the sky and stood up and said, "Come, have some berries and mushrooms. And she paused as she walked closer to her husband, while smiling at him.

Anna and Joseph hugged tight and the children surrounded them. Joseph said, "let us hold hands and dance and Anna nodded, and they danced until they could no longer dance and they lay where they had danced panting for breath, while their faces were beet red. The sun shone bright upon them in a funnel-like radiance clear through the intermingled branches of trees and leaves, which were higher than seven feet tall. They lay staring in wonder—breathing in the free and pristine air, blotting out the terror that was real and that surrounded them and was ready to gobble them up. "How to survive", was the thought that ran through Joseph Freier's mind, and he squinted through his thick glasses and shook both fists several times and then looked up to the sun and then bowed his head. His heart ached for his former way of life; his heart ached for all of the people that he knew. His heart ached for all of his nephews and nieces, brother and sisters, and for Anna's family. Anna, he thought was one of eleven children. One brother, Ben, had already gone to the United States and he met a young woman, who was a nurse and he married her. Anna's youngest brother, Eleazar, had been smuggled out of Czechoslovakia and had made it to Israel. He thought to himself, "at least two are safe". He paused for a moment and smelled the running water, which was hidden from sight because there was a huge rock in the front of it. "Come", he said softly, as he extended his hand to Anna and helped her up from the forest ground. "We will go back to the house", he said. Anna bit her lip and hesitated and then spoke, "but will we be safe from the Nazis?" Joseph explained, "Frank and I visited with Bernard, and it is all set. Come let us go". They walked slowly and gracefully fitting in with the mood of the forest. It was nighttime and the nighttime air already was foreboding of a cold and bitter winter.

CHAPTER 6

WE HAVE BECOME A NEW PEOPLE
AND A RENEWED PEOPLE

No one spoke about the neighbors who were gone, but the thought was there in their minds. Those who remained were forbidden to worship in the Temples. The men and women gathered secretly in homes of people they could trust and made a list of where and when they would hold prayer services. Prayers and services continued in Micholovce during the beginning and until the end of the war. Those who remained had special permission from the Nazis to stay because of their businesses; they were designated as needed for the German cause. Frank had gone to Bernard again on behalf of Joseph Freier and his family. He had asked that Joseph and his family be allowed to stay in Micholvce. Joseph had to sign over the business to Frank and Joseph became Frank's foreman.

We heard stories of men and women who had escaped from the back of trucks. There were vivid and terrifying stories of the Nazi machines, which were used at the gas chambers. There were stories also told of waking up in the depths of dead lying in deep pits. Some told us of the untold horrors they faced in the woods while hiding, and of the dying from disease, pestilence, and the dying from hunger in the woods. Few survived this torturous existence. And in the absence of any worshiping to God because it was forbidden, those victims of untold atrocities still kept their faith. We still kept our faith and believed more in our Judaism.

This time we were lucky. We did not lose this game of ultimate death with the Germans. After a few days, my father took Sam and they wandered in the dark by themselves, knocking on doors to see who amongst us had survived. We had all lived near one another. After the atrocities, no one knew who lived next to whom.

Others had managed to elude the Germans, too. We renewed our ties with friends and neighbors and family members with tears of joy and seemingly endless stories of survival. Our thirst for revenge was sizzling in all of us, but there was the sense of hopelessness of not knowing how to fight. We were not trained. The few of us who had been drafted into the Russian army had never held prominent positions. We as Jews were always limited by the Russian Cossacks and the Tsar. But from all the years of persecution, and revolts against us, we had developed an untenable will of resistance to survive.

The trees all were clothed with leaves and we saw the buds of new vegetation still busting through the earth. We sang praises to the Lord by reciting verses of one of the verses of King David's psalms. After hours of steady walking, our mouths were parched from thirst and our bellies ached from hunger. We had not yet learned to deal with the extreme deprivation on our bodies in times of stress and in times of warfare and took a dangerous chance of walking out of the woods and going back to our home.

The first thing we saw was people walking in the streets. This was our biggest surprise. Houses had open windows. All doors were closed. A small light could be seen shining from inside some of the homes. The neighborhood at first looked untouched by war, in that most of the homes were intact. But the silence in some of the homes was eerie and foreboding. There were telltale signs of unpacked suitcases, coats that had fallen off of beds, sweaters that were piled high on kitchen chair; and rotting food in the back yards of homes; and trash and broken glass in the front of some others. We knew that these people must have had contacts and money. We prayed for those poor people who didn't.

All these sights indicated to the observer that shattering events were taking place. Yet, the items lay so still as though just recently uncovered by gentle hands, sifting from the sands of time in another time by a dedicated archeologist. I wanted to go back to the days when I walked with my brothers to school. Sam would always invite friends over and they would eat cake left outside on a counter for them; gulping the huge morsels in their mouths; not even washing off the bits and crumbs left on their lips and just barely flapping off the crumbs from their shirts; energized, they ran to the backyard to play soccer; they played one game after another; it was nighttime before they stopped and went home. Sam was bright but never a good student. The game and winning the game was the reason why.

Life somehow went on. We found the way to work. The children found a way to learn even though they had to stay at home. For we had the message from God telling us to have tenacity and to go on; we were determined to live. We had some money stored away. Where was the money hidden? It was pasted behind the wallpaper. My father's wood business was being run by his foreman. My father always knew that he could get money from his foreman when he needed the money. That was the bitter irony in this war. Some people were good and they never changed and they became better people, more responsible people. Others were bad and they became worse. Men and women were either overcome by the war. Many took their own lives. Some tried to save themselves and others, risked their lives time after time. Some thought only about themselves; they were cunning with schemes to survive at the expense of anyone. They had never before become so ruthless. Many were in denial----made it worse and their fate was decided in most cases very quickly by the Germans.

We heard stories of men and women who had escaped from the back of trucks. There were vivid and terrifying stories of the Nazi machines, which were used at the gas chambers. There were stories also told of waking up in the depths of the dead lying in deep pits. Some told us of the untold horrors they faced in the woods while hiding, and of the people dying from diseases, pestilence, and the dying from hunger. Few survived this torturous existence. And in the absence of any worshiping to God because it was forbidden, those victims of untold atrocities still kept their faith. We still kept our faith and believed more in our Judaism.

This time we were lucky. We did not lose this game with the Germans today. After a few days, my father took Sam and they wandered through the neighborhood by themselves, knocking on doors to see who amongst the many of us had survived. Yes, others amongst us had managed to elude the Germans, too. We renewed our ties with friends and neighbors and family members with tears of joy and seemingly endless stories of survival.

The thirst for revenge was sizzling in all of us, but there was the sense of hopelessness of not knowing how to mobilize an army. We were not trained as a group for fighting. The many of us who had been drafted into the Russian army had never held prominent positions. Many of us never came back. We as Jews were always limited by the Russian Cossacks and the Tsar. However, we had seen how they had trained their armies, how they mobilized, how they transported their armies, how they stored their supplied, how they obtained their supplied; we were not entirely ignorant. But, how, who will do this and who will pay for that and who will implement that---there was so much planning to be done and we did not have any time to do it. We had to fight and we had to fight as soon as possible. But from all the years of persecution, and revolts against us, we had developed an untenable will of resistance to survive. This was besides our peaceful way of life.

CHAPTER 7

JOSEPH WORKING AND ANNA DELIVERING BABIES

New wallpaper was pasted and many of the rooms had money pasted on the inside of the wallpaper. But the heart and soul of the family was constantly thinking about G-d. No one knew what would happen on the next day. As time went on, Joseph as well as many others talked of being able to warn each other when the Germans came. It was harder than ever to send out an alert for there weren't that many Jews left on the block anymore.

Martin caught more colds than the other children. He was at home more. He helped his mother to cook. He helped his mother to clean the house. He helped his mother gather and carry the groceries when she went to shop, even though all food was rationed. Thoughts of hunger and fear of being captured hovered over them; but, nevertheless, life went on. Jewish people married. Babies were born. Anna was a midwife.

There was a knock on the door in the middle of the night—it was the middle of March and the winter was still stiff and bitter cold, but there were some signs of the new buds on the leaves of the trees. Joseph tied the straps in a knot in the front of his maroon colored flannel robed, the strap on the lap swinging up and obscuring the yellow star, which every Jew had to sew onto their clothes, but only for a moment, but it reminded Joseph to have more faith and he ran down the stairs quickly and asked as he spoke through the thick, wooden brown door, "what is it?"

A voice of a young man shouted, "Help me. My wife needs a midwife". Joseph opened the door and said to the young man whom he had known since he was born, "Schmul, please sit down, and I will get Anna".

Anna had heard the young man's plea, and she had gotten dressed, and had brought her bag. She came down the steps dressed in her best dress and wearing a kerchief to cover her head. Joseph and Anna looked at each other. She said to Joseph, "I will just put on my coat and take my bag". Joseph said, "Be safe". Anna nodded with her head, and she went with Schmul.

It was a distance, around 10 blocks, around the other side of the synagogue and this night was very dark. "Would you like me to light a match?" Schmul asked. "Better not to", Anna quipped. Do you want the Germans to see us?" Schmul rubbed his mouth with his left hand and said with a voice that was noticeably quivering, "what a time to bring a baby into the world". Anna said to him as they walked briskly in the front of the homes along the road, "you must never question the will of the Lord for he is the giver of life".

Schmul looked up at her and said, "Maybe there is hope, but I do not think we will survive this war". Anna quickly retorted, "You are young and you are brave. After the baby is well enough, you must leave. You do know that. "But how?" he asked. And he said, "We have no money". Anna told him, "it will not be easy, but you must find out who is leaving and ask if you can go along with them".

Schmul replied, "I will do as you say". They were fast approaching the home. It was built as a small house, but several rooms were built in the back, and all of the rooms inside were very neat. A lady who lived next door had come over to help, even though she kept on looking up at the clock and batting her eyes and wringing her fingers. She made everyone else nervous.

Anna asked the young woman, laying on the bed whose face was full of perspiration, "what is your name", and while breathing puffs of air in and out and crying, she muttered the name, "Rose". "Oh, what a beautiful name you have". Then Anna paused and she asked how far apart are the contractions?" and Rose replied in a hurried voice, "one and one/half minutes". "Then I would suggest you move your feet closer to me and let me see if I can see if the baby's head coming".

Rose screamed out as Anna felt for the baby's head. Anna spoke quietly to the young man, and she went back quickly into Rose's room. She said, "Rose, look at me. You will come through this. I have been through this five times myself, and I have beautiful children. They make my world", and she muttered to herself, "If the Nazis do not destroy it", and she said slowly, "I will have to turn the baby around, and you will have to help me".

"Here", she said, as she pulled out a small bottle of vodka from her bag. Rose pulled her head up from the huge, duck feather pillow she had been resting on, and she opened up her mouth and Anna poured in droplet by droplet from a large silver tablespoon. Rose rested her head on the pillow, and Anna deftly placed her hands around the baby's head and neck and shoulders and very carefully turned the little body around. Rose had dozed off, but Anna woke her up and said, "come on, push, and Rose gave a large push and the baby's head moved out of the internal crest it had been nesting on. Anna looked at Rose and said, "Rose, you can do it, now give one more push", and Rose did just that and as the head of the newborn baby came out of Rose's womb, Anna grabbed hold of the shoulders and pulled the baby out ever so gently. Rose was dazed, but looked fondly at the baby. The baby lay down on its bed and the neighbor woman covered Rose and said, "there, now, do not worry about the baby", and you will be fine", and Rose nodded her head as if to say, "yes". Rose could hear the baby crying out loudly. Anna had held up the baby by its legs and had slapped its bottom and as the baby was crying, she washed the newborn with the warm water and soap in the basin that had been placed by the side of the bed. She wrapped warm diapers around its bottom, and she wrapped its young, beautiful body into a rainbow colored cloth made of wool. She called out, "it is a boy. It is a boy". She said to Rose, "here, here is your son. Take him and hold him". Rose smiled and she reached out for her baby son. Anna said, "To have wonderful things happen during a war is a wonderful thing".

She wrapped her kerchief around her head and tied it under her neck and put her arms through the inside of the coat, and she said, "My, it is late. I must be going". She walked out into the cold and damp air, but stopped for a minute to look up to the sky and breathe in the air. Then she checked to make sure that all of her buttons had been buttoned and she pulled the right side of the collar over the left side.

She had gone only a few steps out the door, when she turned around and said to the lady neighbor, "it might be best if you and I stayed for the night", and she paused and then said in a serious tone of voice, "just in case there is bleeding".

After breakfast the next morning, seeing Rose and the baby were doing fine, she left and was out the door as though she had disappeared. She bowed her head and walked swiftly past one house and then another. She had gone about half the distance, when she paused and looked around, as she pondered, "What is the fastest way to go to my house". She decided to walk behind the houses, because it was safer, but she would have to walk slower, because she did not know her way as well. She walked while her breathing got louder and she could see the condensation of the air blowing out of her lips and her nostrils. She wanted to stop and rest, but she said to herself, "it is a miracle that I have made it this far, oh, if only I can make it back to the house safely!" and she continued on her way. Two lights shined from the distance, and she knew instantly who they were. She looked up to the sky for strength, and she found the strength to be elusive.

She chuckled to herself as she said, "I certainly know better than to ask them for help"! They will help me all right, but to the grave sooner than I want to go". She darted in the back of the nearest bushes. The lights got brighter and brighter, and with every moment that passed Anna's breathing got heavier. She waited for them to pass. The car crept by slowly. It crept passed this house. Then it went on. Anna thought to herself, "better to wait for a while after they have gone", and she was right! The car turned around and the lights moved closer and closer from the other direction. Anna's breathing got even louder and she could hear the pounding of her heart, and her fists were clenched across the bottom of her chin. She waited. She waited and then the car passed by slowly. She waited for a few minutes longer, got up and arched her back and breathed in deeply and breathed out again and again until she felt that her strength had returned and she walked, one foot before the other, walked briskly passed two more blocks of houses, and, finally, approached the back door of her home and knocked gently.

Sam, the eldest son, had been waiting for her. He moved the curtain a tiny bit from the edges of the window and peered out. He smiled as he saw his mother and went immediately to the back door and opened it up. Anna's face was ruddy and she did not speak, but she rubbed her hands together and walked over to the fireplace and closed her eyes for a moment as she felt the warmth from the fire pumping through her veins.

"Come", her son called her name very gently, "come and sip some hot coffee". She walked quickly to the kitchen table and pulled out a chair for herself. She sipped the hot coffee that had sat in the pot for at least four hours and she smacked her lips, showing what she was too tired to express. She asked for a piece of bread or a piece of cake. Sam obligingly went to get it for her.

Life somehow went on. For we had the spirit of God telling us to have tenacity and to go on; we were determined to live. We had some money stored away. My father's wood business was being run by his foreman.

My father always knew that he could get money from his foreman if he needed the money. That was the bitter irony in this war. Some people were good and they never changed and they became better, more responsible people. Others were bad and they became worse. Men and women were either overcome by the war. Many took their own lives. Some tried to save themselves and others, risked their lives time after time. Some thought only about themselves. They were cunning with schemes to survive at the expense of anyone. They had never before become so ruthless. Many were in denial----made it worse and their fate was decided in most cases very quickly by the Germans.

We heard stories of men and women who had escaped from the back of trucks. There were vivid and terrifying stories of the Nazi machines, which were used at the gas chambers. There were stories also told of waking up in the depths of dead lying in deep pits. Some told us of the untold horrors they faced in the woods while hiding, and of the dying from disease, pestilence, and the dying from hunger in the woods. Few survived this torturous existence. And in the absence of any worshiping to God because it was forbidden, those victims of untold atrocities still kept their faith. We still kept our faith and believed more in our Judaism.

This time we were lucky. We did not lose this game of ultimate death with the Germans. After a few days, my father took Sam and they wandered in the dark by themselves, knocking on doors to see who amongst us had survived. We had all lived near one another. After the atrocities, no one knew who lived next to whom.

Others had managed to elude the Germans, too. We renewed our ties with friends and neighbors and family members with tears of joy and seemingly endless stories of survival. Our thirst for revenge was sizzling in all of us, but there was the sense of hopelessness of not knowing how to fight. We were not trained. The few of us who had been drafted into the Russian army had never held prominent positions. We as Jews were always limited by the Russian Cossacks and the Tsar. But from all the years of persecution, and revolts against us, we had developed an untenable will of resistance to survive.

The trees all were clothed with leaves and we saw the buds of new vegetation still busting through the earth. We sang praises to the Lord by reciting verses of one of the verses of King David's psalms. After hours of steady walking, our mouths were parched from thirst and our bellies ached from hunger. We had not yet learned to deal with the extreme deprivation on our bodies in times of stress and in times of warfare and took a dangerous chance of walking out of the woods and going back to our home.

The first thing we saw was people walking in the streets. This was our biggest surprise. Houses had open windows. All doors were closed. A small light could be seen shining from inside some of the homes. The neighborhood at first looked untouched by war, in that most of the homes were intact. But the silence in some of the homes was eerie and foreboding. There were telltale signs of unpacked suitcases, coats that had fallen off of beds, sweaters that were piled high on kitchen chair; and rotting food in the back yards of homes; and trash and broken glass in the front of some others. We knew that these people must have had contacts and money. We prayed for those poor people who didn't.

All these sights indicated to the observer that shattering events were taking place. Yet, the items lay so still as though just recently uncovered by gentle hands, sifting from the sands of time in another time by a dedicated archeologist. I wanted to go back to the days when I walked with my brothers to school. Sam would always invite friends over and they would eat cake left outside on a counter for them; gulping the huge morsels in their mouths; not even washing off the bits and crumbs left on their lips and just barely flapping off the crumbs from their shirts; energized, they ran to the backyard to play soccer; they played one game after another; it was nighttime before they stopped and went home. Sam was bright but never a good student. The game and winning the game was the reason why.

When we reached the steps to our home, we could have collapsed right there and then. We practically pummeled down the door. But after looking at the walls in the house and the furniture, we realized that everything that we owned had a special story. We had earned and had never taken anything. We realized when inside that we were free. We were inside. We were behind locked doors, but we felt free. In the woods with all of the land around us, we did not feel that we owned anything.

Our strength, our physical strength and our endurance to put up with the unknown and the disposal of the Nazis returned, but anger against the Nazis surfaced. You could see our bitterness on the expressions on our faces. Silently, I asked the questions, "Why had the Germans learned to hate us so and was the reason for their hate so strong that they had a right to take us as their prisoners? Would any of the other people in the van survive? We all cried and we grimaced, showing our feelings. We talked. My father said, "Only fear God and not the Germans". I asked, 'But they want to kill us". My father answered, "But you must find the strength to escape from their grasp. We must survive. "Do you hear what I say?" He raised his voice? "Do you hear what I say?" I shuddered, but I was the first one to answer the question, "Yes".

He said to all of us, "Well, then, we have had quite a time of it, and I think that tomorrow will bring a new day for us and then there is the Sabbath. We all went upstairs to our bedrooms to sleep. There were no suitcases to unpack. We had left the suitcases and had fled. My father told us in the morning "that he was going to make a plan so that we all do not get captured at the same time". He said, "If one or two of us escapes, then we can help the others". It made sense.

CHAPTER 8

VIGILANCE AND CLEVERNESS

One day Henry alerted us that one man was coming. He was coming solo, alone, and he was walking. The man, dressed in a dusty, tattered pair of brown pants that looked like it had many owners, and a sweater which had shed badly and had some patches of wool on the arms parts, walked in from what looked like the burning of the sun, a Hell which not one of us should want to go through. His shoes were burrowing in the ground as though his feet were too tired to go another step, but some spirit from within him was propelling him, as if from the ages; he must have walked about one-hundred miles or more.

He came to tell us that the Germans had come to his town, had rounded up as many of the Jews as they were able to fit in their trains, and then they were off with their unlucky prey to their extermination camps. My father and other men offered him wine and pieces of cake. The man sat on the ground with his feet outstretched making the soles on the bottom of his soles an object of everyone's sense of observation and pity for the man.

He sloped and slurped up the food as though there was no tomorrow, stopping occasionally to drink some wine in-between. Men from the crowd called out, "Take it slower", but the man was ravenous. He asked someone in the crowd as he pulled on his arm, asking, "Could you give him a piece of bread?" He was given several pieces of bread. The bread he quickly stashed in his jacket pocket, and then he wiped the drippings from his nose in a ragged piece of cloth, and the running tears from his eyes, and crying, he called out, "They took my wife and my three daughters".

"I", he muttered, became separated from them. I was to wait with others for another train.

When I saw no Germans nearby, I ran behind a tree and hid, praying in my hands as I waited each moment, each stepping sound, for the walking crowd to go away. Darkness came. Others did the same. We ran in all directions. Then I ran as fast as I could for miles in the woods and when I could no longer catch my breath, I hid under some brush and I must have slept for days". I awoke with a sharp 'startle' as a rabbit made a jump over me".

My father asked him, "What can I do to save my family and other people?" The man winced from nervous exhaustion, as he answered, "It is told", he said in words which rambled on and on, and then finally, "that if you can find a priest who will give you Christian papers, you will not be considered as a Jew". The man was then too tired to continue talking and was taken to someone's home.

People who had gathered to listen to the man in the town square went home to their families. My father came home and said to Anna and asked, "We will need $200.00 to pay a priest in the Catholic Church for Christian papers". Anna went upstairs. She did not hesitate. She put the cash in the palm of Joseph's hand, and he put the money quickly in the inside of his jacket pocket.

He called loudly: while breathing in several puffs of breath, "Sam, Martin, I need you both to come with me to the Catholic Church in town". Facing the church was a new experience for us, but we had always gotten along with Catholic people. My father walked in first. Sam followed, but at a distance, but he never let his eyes wander from his father. Martin followed Sam. Martin's mind wandered to the usual Christmas scene that was always displayed in the town. It was always festive and people were always shopping for gifts, and the children were always following their parents and laughing and playing with toys and their friends or siblings.

It was already the middle of winter and soon, Martin was thinking, the carolers will go from house to house to sing. Those of us in the ghetto would always listen to hear them, the carolers, singing in the distance. The big church in town would open its doors and the light from the brightness inside would glow brightly and extend into the distance. Even though the church was alien to us, we nevertheless felt its warmth from time to time.

It was late at night, about 10 o'clock when we came to the front door. Sam pulled at the handle of the metal, horse-shoe-shaped knocker. A voice from the depths of the halls answered, "I am coming". We waited so impatiently for the door to open, counting the seconds as though they were giant minutes. A tall, stout man, dressed in the garb of a black top, and black pants stood at the inside of the door.

For a moment, we stared at the Priest and he stared back at us. It was almost as though he had the same fears that we had. Joseph moved forward, relaxed a bit and, smiled a little, feeling relaxed after seeing the Priest. Martin was thinking to himself, "Will this Priest help us or call the Gestapo", but he did not flinch or indicate his thoughts. Sam positioned himself so that if he had to run, he would. Sam stood directly behind Joseph.

The Priest looked all around us. Then he quickly motioned, "Come. Come in". We walked quickly through the large open archway in the indoor hallway. The Priest closed the door behind us while he searched again for any movement outside. He bolted the door and then clapped his hands, "Gentlemen, he said, "I know why you are here". Joseph nodded his head in agreement, "Then you know that we have come to buy passports". "Yes", and I will explain, he said as the walls resounded with the echoes of the voices of the men. "Let me help you by telling you that we have assigned a scribe to print passport papers for you all". And he hesitated and asked in a soft voice, "Do you have the $200.00? My father nodded his head. "Okay then, I will take the money", and Joseph undid the buttons of his jacket and reached for his inner pocket and pulled out the money. Joseph cleared his throat and handed over the money to the priest.

The silence of voices and sounds was both shattering and chilling. It was as though there was a stopping of time. After that moment of silence, within me was the whirlwind of time, of the centuries of history gone by, and the centuries of history to be. I wanted to enter the funnel in my mind, and spirit, and spirit, and body; and leave this time zone. My hands started to shake.

My father had a look of uncertainty on his face. Sam was the instant soldier; he looked ready to fight. The silence of the centuries was interrupted by the voice of the Priest. He explained, "There is a wooden house in the back of the church. Remember to knock three times and then wait for a man to call out, "What number you be?" And say the number one and then say the word, sanctuary". The Priest paused and looked into our eyes, and said, "I feel for you people". And he hesitated and asked the question, "What number you be?" There were tears in Joseph eyes, but he did not reach into his pocket for a handkerchief. Joseph answered softly, "one".

The Priest went to the front door and the three of us walked out and walked down the path which was on the side of the church. The pebbles got into our feet. Ivy draped the corners of the wall. Holly bushes dotted the long exterior of the building with bright red berries dotting the strong, deep verdant colored leaves. We descended down the slope to the back of the church and then walked up a steep hill to a large brown, wooden house with a large brown wooden door.

My father knocked gently and a voice from the distance called out, "Coming, coming". Our knees seemed shattered and the ground was unusually soft where we stood, almost too soft, ready to swallow us up. A voice called out, "What number you be?" My father cleared his throat and answered, "number one". No sound. Martin prompted Joseph, "Say the word, sanctuary", and Joseph muttered the word loud enough for the priest to hear.

The door swung open, as a short, stout man with a priest's attire said, "Come in. I was expecting you". With our eyes wide open and our breathing noticeably loud, we stared at the man in sameness as though we were triplets. "Well, come in, come in", he said to us as he fanned the fingers of his hands towards himself and stood up in a squatting motion. The door slammed quickly behind us and shut out half of the natural light, but we were not in darkness. We could not speak. The man stared at us with his large pitch black eyes and then smiled and said, "What are your names, all seven of you?" The man who was a monk artistically crafted our names on the documents and when he was finished, my father shook his hand and thanked him.

We boys, Sam and I, Martin, at an aged sense of maturity, understood the full meaning of what the Priest and the Monk had done for us. They had given us a chance to survive the terrible onslaught of hate that had befallen my people. They had allowed us to join their congregation. It was good of them. If the situation was reverse, I think we Jews would have done the same good deed for them.

It is true that the papers meant conversion to Catholicism, but our main purpose was to survive. We were assured that God in his infinite wisdom had a specific and enriching purpose for us after this war was over. As we exited the front door of the monk's study, the monk said softly, "Better to walk a mile in the back and then you will see a road. The road leads you right into town. I asked, "How long will it take us?" The monk replied, "One-half an hour to one hour. Now come on now. Hurry along so that I can look to my preserves".

We smiled. The road back home was difficult—ravines covered most of the pathway and we found ourselves crawling under the thick underbrush at times. Other times, we found ourselves fighting the thorns on the wild raspberries dried stalks, stalks which caught us and clung to us while we were trying to walk over the stalks. But my father knew about being in the woods so we never panicked.

With torn pants and ruffled jackets and blood oozing all over our fingers, we left the sanctity of the woods and walked into the muck and mire of the panic, the square of the town; our fears for survival heightened as we knew that the storm of the Nazis was a maelstrom in which so many had already disappeared. We hoped that the conversion would last for a while so that we could make final plans to escape from Czechoslovakia.

Anna was excited to see us when we got home. We passed out the passports and sat down at the dinner table and feasted on buckwheat pancakes and onions. Then we talked about acting as Christians. "You must follow everything that the others do", my father said. Edith said, "But I want to be a Jew". My father answered, "You are being a Jew by surviving the Nazis. We all went to sleep early that night. We were grateful we had money coming in from our wood business. We were grateful to have food for another day. In the morning, my father and I would walk to the house where the Rabbi was living and we would speak about helping others by giving money and food.

We came to church occasionally. We would go to one of the morning masses. I was surprised at how easily I learned the hymns and the Latin words. We were, however, always Jews. Our hearts and souls and thinking were always about our history and our holidays and our prayer services. The war had taken a lot away from us. We missed the peacefulness of the Sabbath and remembered the preparation for the Sabbath—the rolling of the dough for the Sabbath bread was always fun. We missed the aroma of chicken soup throughout the whole house. I could taste the soup in my mouth, but I knew that it was not real. What a nice festive celebration we had every Friday night and Saturday. It was peaceful; it was the very opposite of this war; this war had robbed us of our peace, of our traditions, and now it was robbing us of our religion. We fought back the tears of remembrance. We tried to remember our prayers. We prayed silently to ourselves many times during the day. This gave us a little respite from this awful situation that we knew was lethal.

We appreciated all that the Priest had done for us. He had shown us that even in a treacherous war that some people are true to their vows and can be good to all people. But on my mind all the time was the question, "How can we go to a church and enjoy its services while Jews are being killed in the extermination camps?" How can we enjoy all the splendor of vibrant colors, mosaics, and painted ceilings in a building that is safe from harm while others are dying such a horrible death?" We felt guilty that other Jews were not as lucky and large numbers of the Jews were dying every day". I, Martin, could not answer this question. I coughed after getting too wrapped up in this thought. I said to myself, "I had better stop thinking". And I paused and bit my tongue as I said to myself, "deny it is all happening. As my mother told me, "Maybe that way it will get better".

In late 1943, it was harder than ever for Jews in Nazi occupied Czechoslovakia to survive. Before the war, our community was looked upon by many communities with awe. Our people had become successful businessman. Jews in Czechoslovakia owned homes, vast acres of woods, and had become doctors, lawyers, teachers, successful businessmen in all businesses. Now, many of us had become Catholics or Christians in order to evade the grasp of the conquering armies of the Nazis. But now, this failed. According to the Germans, all Jews were to be eradicated from the world. A museum was to be set up in their honor.

Over these few years, we had lost our community of people. It had taken us centuries to build. Now we were forced to hide for our lives. Events proved to get a lot worse in the war. The Slovakian partisans wanted to fight to the death to retake their country in late August of 1944. They planned a rebellion and their army was made up of many Slovak army officers who had gone over to the Russian army or who had escaped to the British Isles and were pilots for the British. Joining them were groups from the Communist party and many thousands of Jewish partisans who were ready to die for the cause of liberating their country from the Nazis. This was a rebellion against the tight-fisted and anti-Jewish regime of Jozef Tiso, the Catholic Priest, who was the Nazi puppet. Participating in the fighting were Jewish fighters from the Jewish labor camps at Novaky, Sered, and Vyhne. It was the hope that by vanquishing the Nazis and the Nazi sympathizers that the remaining 20,000 Jews that remained in Slovakia would be spared from the death and throes of the war.

Joseph shook his head back and forth. He said, "It is a wonder that we are all alive". Anna with wide eyes said, "The Lord has given us life when so many others are dying at the hands of the Germans. But, Joseph, your cunning has saved us so many times". The boys all acknowledged. "What are we doing about food?" Questioned Martin, as he cleared his throat.

Joseph cleared his throat and said, "Well, at the moment, we are living on what we find, scrounging around the town". Sometimes, if you are lucky the bakery is open in the early hours of the day. "Well, there are seven of us now and the food will soon be gone", Sam stated. "Yes, you are right to be thinking of food", said Joseph, "and I will see if my foreman will bring in some food for us".

"But what will we do with ourselves?" cautioned Edith, as she leaned on the right heal of her foot and held her hands on her waistline". Anna finished the question, "you can clean the house with me or you can read one of the books we have managed to hide". Edith snorted, but kept quiet, because she did not wish to upset her relationship with her mother. Joseph waited for his turn to talk and then interjected, "the boys can cut wood with me". He looked at the boys for their approval and saw sour expressions on their faces. Knowing this, he said, we can always play a game of chess and he saw each of the boys smile. He knew that he had to find the chess boards and he did.

Amidst papers strewn all over the dirt roads, and the cracked and jagged cement walks, and open suitcases left abandoned in the street, and burned out homes, and homes with broken doors, and broken windows, and abandoned children roaming aimlessly throughout the streets, and the dying, and the dead stretched-out with rigor mortis, and the panic seen in the eyes of everyone whom Joseph passed on the road, he went to work every day.

He would tuck inside his jacket any leftover bread, cheese, or meat. Occasionally, a large sack of potatoes was delivered to the factory and he stuffed his pockets with the brown-colored golden eggs. Everyone grabbed onions immediately. Still it was better than waiting in line for rations. The yellow star burned deep into the fibers of his jacket and into the sinews of his heart. He mumbled to himself day after day, "what to do. What can I do?" He shook his head.

Another year went by and no end to the war. Rumors heard at work. Rumors heard on the street. A friend or relative would occasionally stop by and talk and say, "it is a little bit too quiet....Mark my words. Something is going to happen. Something big is going to happen!"

CHAPTER 9

THE TRAIN

Joseph looked out the window, shielding himself behind the ochre colored lace curtain. More people were in the streets than ever. More and more people passed the house. Joseph thought to himself, "Where are all of these people going and why?" People hurried. People ran with suitcases. People ran with babies in one arm and a child in the other. Joseph called to Anna. He said to her with a tone in his voice of concern, "take a look outside". She watched while standing by his side. Joseph said to her, "Go quickly. We must pack too. We must leave too."

Joseph got out of bed quicker than usual the next day. He threw his blanket back quickly and with the bottoms of both feet not yet warmed by the lack of circulation flowing as he walked across the large, rectangular bedroom floor which was covered with a most distinguishable handmade, woolen rug, which immediately caught the eye of the viewer by its four matching blue colors. He darted to the window. "I hear a noise in the distance", he muttered to himself, as he scratched at his brow. He tugged hard, unconsciously, at the clear white lace curtain, as he peered in all directions of the town with the simultaneous roving of both of his eyes. He could see in the far distance what looked like the rounded head of a pin. It was coming--quickly and it was getting bigger and bigger. His hand released the curtain and shook and then he called, "Anna, get the children, the Germans are practically here.

Anna got dressed as she tugged at the bottom of her dress and grimaced with a determination to survive at whatever had to be done. She muttered to herself, "I cannot let them take the children", and she ran to the older boys' large bedroom door and called out, "Sam and Bernard", get dressed quickly, and she darted off to the large bedroom down the hall and yelled, "Martin, wake up your younger brother, Henry, and come quickly". "Is it the Germans", Martin called out with a pointed deep questioning voice," and she answered quickly in no uncertain terms. "Yes, it is the Germans. They have come for the Jews, and his eyes, the young eyes of an 11 year-old looked into the deep black colored eyes of his mother and he saw that she was afraid.

He got out of the bed and woke up his 9-year old brother, Henry. He said, "Henry, you must wake up, and he shook him gently until Henry opened his eyes and muttered the few short words, "what is happening"? Martin quickly responded, "come quickly, we must all go downstairs to be with father". Anna followed the four boys down the stairs and she held onto Edith's hand tightly and led her down the stairs. Edith wept uncontrollably. Anna hugged her and patted her oldest child's hair off of the front of her face and said, "We shall survive. We shall overcome this", and Edith whimpered for a few seconds and then stopped crying and sat mute. They sat in the kitchen and all waited.

Fears, unfortunately, sometimes they come true. Our biggest fear was that the Germans would come for us again and take us to the train. The train, was the infamous word; we could not even mention the word; the word brought tears; the word brought panic; it brought the infamous reality of the long, long ride to somewhere out in the wilderness, with guards, armed with rifles and barbed wired fences, and crowded rooms, and starvation rations, and work, work all day and practically all night---all hard labor.

It had been a cold misty night; one of those weeks at the end of spring where the weather kind of wants to spin around and around and decide should it go back to spring, summer, winter, or fall, or nearly, and then somehow rights itself. The riders came this time late in the night. Very few people heard their evil call. Joseph heard them. He knew. He told Anna that he was going to his foreman's house and that he would be back as soon as he was able. Anna said, "Isn't it dangerous?" "They are not here yet. I will be back in time".

He knew the way and he walked quickly. He reached the house in fifteen minutes, record time for he had to leave the ghetto and go into the town. Most people knew who he was and no one wanted to make him trouble. Most people felt sorry for his plight. His foreman was up early and saw him coming and opened up the door for him immediately, looking with a watchful eye and closed the door quickly. "What can I do for you, Joseph?" the foreman asked.

Joseph breathed in and out and blurted out, "the Germans are coming and this time they mean to take us all on the train". "What can I do to help you," the

foreman asked?" "Please" and Joseph could hardly stand straight on his feet, and he pleaded, "You must go now to the German Commandant and ask him to release me and my family". "Yes, I will go right now".

Joseph pried open the door, looked in every direction and walked quickly for dear life. His foreman put on his jacket, put his key into his pants pocket and pulled his jacket collar over his ears, put on his leather cap, and left the house. He knew exactly what building to go to.

Joseph hurried along. A few more people were walking in the streets. This worried Joseph a little, because there was always the worry of a policeman on the street or of an undercover Nazi, but he walked quickly and kept his head down, never looking at anyone, never attracting any attention.

It was an hour later, but Joseph had made excellent time; and he was inside his home sitting at his kitchen table, drinking some hot coffee. Joseph said to Anna, "This time when the Nazis come, we will all have to go together. Don't take any clothing. Pack a nap sack of food for each of us to carry on our backs. An hour passed; then two hours passed. Then they heard noises, clattering and banging noises. Then the noises came closer. Then they heard shouting. Then there was a powerful knocking on the front door and shouting.

Joseph's mind was on how to escape with his family. He knew that escape was only a chance if his foreman would come through with the papers, but he needed more inner strength to fight an evil that was dedicated to the virtual destruction of his people. He prayed silently to himself the words of the Sma prayer, which had been read and chanted for hundreds and hundreds of years. He said to himself with a sense of conviction, "even the Nazis cannot take away my deep faith in h'shem". And he repeated over and over again the verse to himself, "the Lord G-d is one, the Lord G-d is one, the Lord is my G-d, and I have faith".

They could hear the sounds of the sirens blaring, and the loud beat of boots running, and then there was a harsh sound knocking with a rifle butt on the front of the door. A voice of a German soldier shouted and demanded, "You open up these doors. We are here to take all of the Jews".

Joseph opened up the front door and the three soldiers lost their balance and almost fell to the floor. "Come with us", they shouted, as they looked around at the well-crafted china cabinets in the dining room and the striking emerald color of the large couch which circled most of the living room, just about

mesmerized them. They took the few lemon drops we had left for themselves from the candy dish and bit into them with their incisors, chewing hard and lapping quickly with their long tongues. They motioned with their hands as they shouted, "make it quick", and they pointed their rifles toward the front door.

We had barely time to put on our coats and fasten our knap sacks when they pushed us out of the front door. They left the front door wide open, never thinking about closing it. We walked in front of them, single file, of course, and bowing our heads, of course, as though we were the worst criminals. What did we do? We were Jews? And they were Nazis and Nazis detested Jews. "Go in", they shouted, as they opened up the back doors to the odd shaped and ugly colored van.

The tires of their van cringed tight onto the worn dirt pavement, creating dust that blew onto the few openings onto the outside of the cars. A soldier shouted, "Stupid Jews, making us drive to this G-d forsaken place. What will come of us all?" And he slapped his comrade who was sitting next to him on the side of his arm. The soldier sitting next to him, hunched up his shoulders and laughed, "All of the Jews are crazy", and he laughed and laughed, putting his bottle of vodka down on the floor, and rocking his head from left to right as the bottle rocked sideways and back and then rolled off into a crevice of the van.

They stood upright—women, older children, old men, old women, younger children, who just a few years ago were running freely around their yards and thinking of who to play with next---fear of dying was written all over their faces. In the darkness of the van, it intensified their own darkness and they forgot about praying. Together, their bodies moved like pieces of wood---whenever the van turned a corner, they all moved together to that corner's direction. They were totally controlled, even by the force of inertia.

Pebbles that lay scattered sporadically along the narrow roads, unpaved and pressed into light brown dirt that oozed off into dust the moment the thick shoddy tires of the van rode over the dirt. The pebbles were talking their own language. They were telling the soldiers to let these innocent people live, but the soldiers clutched their guns and wallowed in their false and psychotic sick pride, and ignored the meaning behind the sound of the pleading. Joseph Freier's fists were tightly clenched, which had the same meaning.

As a young boy, he had been sent by his father to study in Germany. He sat amongst the other students, and whenever he worked hard and did well on an exam, most of the other students heckled him out of jealousy. He survived and finished his schooling. Now he was running a big lumber business and was the envy of most of the Christians and Jews in the town. He knew what he was doing. He grew to be very successful. He had over 40 employees.

Anna took care of the chores in the house—cooking the cholent all day in the large metal stove, washing the clothes in a large metal wash basin as she rubbed on the rubbing board. She gave birth to a child before every second year. They had one daughter and four sons. Anna was from a family of eleven children. They all lived nearby, with the exception of her older brother, the firstborn. He fell in love with a beautiful Christian girl and they moved to Hungary. Once every year, they received a post card from him. Anna had mostly sisters but the youngest brother was seventeen and his name was Eleazar, a bright young man, resourceful, and when Joseph realized that the Jewish youth were being collected by the Nazis, he suggested strongly to Anna that she help her Eleazar flee to Israel. Eleazar was given the passage money and some money to spare and he boarded a boat that arrived in a port in Israel.

Moments from his courtship of Anna came to his mind. She was already twenty-three and he was twenty-seven. She could cook meatballs that melted in your mouth. She could prepare a full meal in one half hour's time. He asked himself the question, "what would happen to Anna if he was taken away by the Nazis. Sweat from his internal fervor poured from the furrows of his brows. He gripped his fists, closed his eyes, blanked out the scenes of the half-living and the dead in front of him and chanted to himself, "I shall survive". He said the words, "I shall survive and my family will survive", over and over again, and he rocked back and forth, almost falling asleep, and forgetting the sounds of moaning and crying and shouting, and pleading and the pound, pounding sound of the knocks of fists banging on the back doors. Thoughts of bedlam and madness coming from the minds of peaceful people—people driven to despair in fear of losing their lives.

We were Jews. A proud people, and we had a proud heritage.

We walked and talked softly if we were able. It was only a small distance to the train station, where the van would drop us off, but it seemed like an eternity. As we walked, we joined others in their walk to the station until the whole road was saturated with Jews being rounded up. The Nazis were having a field day. The doors swung open to what seemed like an endless number of cars attached to the caboose of the head train. The Nazis herded us in, lifted us in, pushed us in. People shouted, people cried, people lost their luggage, people lost their children----nothing mattered---the Nazis herded them into the cars.

Joseph and his family had been put into one of the end cars, by chance; they stood in the middle of the car, holding each others' hands and closing their eyes. They were convinced that this was the end for them. In the train were a few remaining members of Joseph's family; but in this train, there were over 32 members, close members of Anna's family, sisters, and their families, and her father. They all waited in anticipation for the sound of the wheels to start

churning. At least the heat from the inside would be better once they got going, they thought. The silence was deafening and the suspense was maddening. All at once they heard the sound of a door closing, then another, then another, then others, then many, and then the sound stopped. There was complete silence. Then out of nowhere a loud puff and the engine roared faster and faster and slowly the engineer released the throttle and the wheels began to turn slowly, ever so slowly; but before the wheels could pick up any momentum, there was a slight jar of the wheels and then a bigger and bigger one until the engine sighed and stopped blowing smoke. People lost their balance and caught onto the clothes of others. Everyone wondered, "What is happening?" No one could see outside the train, except for a little break in the wooded structure of the car or a hole, here and there, and it was difficult to determine what was happening.

An officer walked off of the front steps of the last train and watched as a man, running, approached the train. Almost out of breath, he waved his papers and gave them to the soldier, and the soldier took them and read them. "Okay", the soldier said, "Release Joseph Freier, and a soldier went into the car and brought out Joseph Freier. The German officer told Joseph Freier, "You are free to go home". Joseph looked the officer in the face and replied, "I will not go without my family".

The officer studied Joseph's face very carefully for a few minutes but then decided that it was best to let Joseph go back into the train for his family. Joseph found Anna and the children and told them to come with him. Anna told him, "No, I want to go with my family". "Joseph replied, "Come quickly. Your children need you and so do I". The children came with Joseph and Anna

followed. They left the train. They began their walk home. The engine of the train started to crank up again, and after all of the smoke left the air, the sound of the clanging of the wheels no longer could be heard. Only the sight of the moving train could be seen in the distance and the object was growing smaller and smaller as it was getting farther and farther away. The family walked on, but very slowly.

CHAPTER 10

ESCAPE TO THE NEARBY WOODS

The door to the house was open. They walked in and Joseph closed the door behind them. Joseph said, "We shall sleep here tonight, but this is a terrible war, and the Nazis will be back with more vengeance, and we may not be as lucky the next time. Luck has a way of running out. Tomorrow we leave. We will live in the woods." No one said a word. They all knew that Joseph was right. They knew that Joseph had saved their lives thus far.

With tears in her eyes, Anna cried, "but where will we go?" Joseph said, "We will survive. We will live in the woods". Joseph held his wife tightly and kissed her on the forehead and then stepped away and said, "Go get the boys and Edith and let us go!" Anna was packing when she heard the sound of the sirens. She heard the sound of the airplanes. She ran to Joseph and he held her and said, "We must leave now", and he asked her if she understood. She opened her eyes and said with a weak tone of voice, "yes, I understand". They left the suitcases where they were. They grabbed whatever cheese and crackers they could find and one by one they ran. Soldiers were coming to the houses and knocking and yelling, "come outside, Jews".

Joseph knew that they must go a long way into the woods before they would be safe. "Crawl on your bellies", he cried out to Anna. She crawled. He cried out to the boys, "crawl on your bellies or you will be seen". The boys crawled behind their mother and their father. Edith crawled beside her mother and every few minutes had to be coaxed to continue. Joseph gave the word to, "stop when they were at least a mile deep into the woods". He said to Anna and the boys and to Edith, "rest for a few minutes, but we must continue". And he paused, because he could not speak the words that he wanted to utter. Finally, he regained his composure. He said, "We must put distance between ourselves and the devil". Anna's stance of determination returned. She motioned to her sons and to her daughter, "let us go on". They walked through the thick underbrush, virgin land that had never been traveled upon for many, many years. The land was untouched by fears and destruction. Everything was green. Wild flowers bloomed. Birds chirped as they flew from branch to branch. The smell of fresh, pristine water was up ahead. "We can stop here for the night", Joseph said. Joseph motioned for Sam to follow him. They stood on a hill, which overlooked much of the forest. Joseph said, "Do you see even a small cave?"

Sam replied after looking for a while, with the sun beating on him even though the air high up in the forest was much colder for this time of the year. Sam spotted something that looked like a mountain structure and he pointed to it. Joseph said, "That is close by. Let us go and see what it is". It was a small cave. The five of them could hardly fit into the small natural shelter, but they had shelter. They ate the little bit of bread that they brought with them, and they ate it with wild mushrooms that Anna had picked. She had taken a walk along a trail and had found the wild mushrooms and had made a pocket out of the lower half of her skirt. There was plenty to eat. They drank water by using the ladle that Anna had brought with her into the forest.

Joseph laughed and it was contagious. Anna laughed the loudest. Joseph said, "We just need a pot for coffee and we will be all set". What I admired most was that he had within him his own spirited will for survival. It helped to have him by my side. I felt cheered up by him. Yes, Sam was determined to survive. My sister Edith needed his strength. She was always crying. No one would have imagined that she was older than Sam. She had a slight build and looked very frail. She was not able to be a leader. She copied everything that we did.

During the nearly one and one-half years in the woods near Micholovce, Sam and I hunted for foods, like small squirrels. He made traps out of pieces of branches and caught squirrels, sometimes rabbits. The squirrels tasted like paper; the rabbits tasted like paper, too, but with an aftertaste of chicken.

I would go with him many times to search for food. Bernard went with us too. A friendship beyond being brothers evolved between us that that I will always be grateful for. There were few words that could be used to express our friendship for each other. We cared for each other's survival and were ready to give up our lives for each other. It was not discussed, but it was understood. The feeling manifested itself always. We knew that we could only justify ourselves to the angels above; this was like an awakening in the clear blue sky amongst the fringed cumulus cloud, which in my thoughts floated above us.

Sam would bring water to our hideout by carrying the water in a hollow log of wood that he had whittled out by himself; later my father's foreman brought us an old, thick, wrought iron cooking pot and we took turns fetching water in it---the pot was so welcome, but heavy. My mother had tears flowing from her eyes when we gave the pot to her; that was the second time that I saw my mother smile during our time in the woods. You could wonder about the meaning of a worn pot. If you really thought about it, it meant using a comfort that had for the most part been taken away.

My mother gathered berries, or picked quince, or crab apples from the trees. My mother knew how to pick mushrooms which were not poisonous. This food that was delivered and especially in the winter time: this is what saved us. My father's foreman brought us food whenever it was safe to bring the food. Sam and my father knew of a safe rendezvous place in the woods, a clearing, but well hidden at the same time. They would wait, pick up the food, and carry it back to our hideout. If there was too much food to carry, my father and Sam would bury the rest and mark the letter f for Freier on a tree nearby. I would go with them later to retrieve the rest of the food.

One time my father's foreman brought us bags of onions. My mother cut the onions and fried them. She boiled them and then mashed them and then fried them as pancakes. My mother mixed mushrooms with the onions and we ate heartily, many times forgetting the torment and storm of war which wantonly killed people. Once, my father's foreman delivered to us three large sacks of potatoes. He said that the potato crop was particularly good this year. We ate the potatoes with the onions and the mushrooms, and we thanked G-d for our bounty and safety. My father and my brother, Bernard planted the shavings from the potatoes and many times, the earth united with the tubules, and new plant roots evolved, and potatoes formed underneath the ground and a little bit of greenery above the plant.

It was a miracle in the middle of the woods. It was good to see new vegetation and new growth. My mother reminded me of the small garden that we always had in the back of our house. She had grown potatoes, and onions, and peas, and carrots, and beets. All of the plants flourished with her care, and we did not need to go to the market for these fresh foods.

When the food rations were given out by the Nazis, which were so scanty, we could always sneak into the back yard and pull out some of the vegetables and eat a plentiful supply—it was heart rendering. The thought of food that we had on hand was so reassuring.

In the woods, there was the monotony of boredom and the fear of being discovered that we had to contend with. Most of the time, we played chess with my father. We prayed together three times a day. We talked a lot. We talked over our problems. We did what we could do---when we got sick. We were pretty much isolated from people so we did not worry too much about catching colds.

One time I did catch a cold---a real bad one. It was before the winter of 1945. The fall weather had been particularly cold. There were many days when the wind howled like a hungry wolf---relentless howling. With the visibility usually very poor during a cold windy rain storm in Slovakia, it was difficult for us to hunt for food. Our food supply of cans was almost all used up.

We knew not to expect a visit from my father's foreman with a new bag of cans. It would be dangerous for the foreman, and we did not want anything to happen to him. We had to begin rationing our food supply. From the lack of food, we started to weaken. We could see the starvation was robbing us of our strength. The colors of our eyes got darker, almost pitch black and the shape of our eyes grew rounder and more pronounced. We started to lick our lips, trying to moisten the inside dryness in our mouths. My father knew he had to keep us busy to keep our minds off of food. When he thought it was safe to look for food, he asked Sam and me to go with him.

It was snowing heavily, one early winter day; we did not go outside to gather wood. When we cooked we heated up the bunker. Joseph has designed an underground stove with a vent that came out away from the bunker. Unless, it was a very clear day, which was rare, one would think that the smoke was mist, which was rising from the air. Our bunker, being under the ground grew to be very cold. The dampness affected me more than the others. I started to cough. I had trouble breathing and my body became very warm.

CHAPTER 11

SAM'S ADVENTURE

My mother knew she had to do something to save me. She told Sam that he had to go to town to get me medicine. He asked, "Where do I go?" She said, "First you must sell my ring at Mr. Jable's the jeweler. My mother tugged at Sam's jacket, "He is the one who is secretly married to a Jew." She breathed in heavily and said, "Do you remember where his shop was?" Sam paused and answered, "Yes, I do". Then Sam buttoned his jacket and looking at my mother with a serious expression on his face, he asked, "What do I do with the money after I sell the ring?"

"Take it to the doctor in town, Dr. Renna; he will know what to do." And Anna looked at her son with expressions of assurance in her eyes. Sam took an apple and put it in his jacket pocket. He took two cookies and put them in his other pocket, and he climbed out of the bunker. No one followed him along the trail. It was as though Sam had emerged from the hidden parts of the earth or of the forest, and was one of the few men who had survived the war and was searching for other men and women who had survived the war.

The glare from the sunshine obstructed his vision; with his eyes squinting. Favoring his left eye, he continued on his trek through the woods. He tore off a blade of grass and put the end of the stalk in his mouth and chewed on the stalk a little bit. He felt like singing a song, but he knew that it was not safe. So he walked and moved his head to the sound of a beat in his head, back and forth and then again and again. He knew the way to the edge of the forest on that side of the woods for it was very close, nearby to where he would meet his father's foreman who brought the food.

But much in the woods is unseen for even a few feet away for one can easily blend in with the forest's apparel and habitats and never be seen.

Sam knew he had to exit the woods away from this spot and he did. He checked his pocket in his pants to make certain he had not lost the ring. "The ring, the diamond ring", he said over and over again. "I must sell it and take the money to the doctor for medicine". He mumbled, "Poor fellow, my brother Martin, sick with a fever--it is not an easy thing to have".

He stopped rocking his head to the rhythm of the beat and gripped his shoulders, looked around the terrain, and the trees a few times and then felt he was determined to succeed. He was going to help his younger brother. He spotted some smoke ahead. His instincts told him, "Look at what is happening, but proceed cautiously". But then other scrambled thoughts clicked on and off in his mind, "Should I run?" He sat down and rocked himself. He rocked as though he was sitting in the synagogue. He prayed and held his hand on his warm forehead, and slowly, he recited the words, "God is one…." He breathed in a deep sigh and remained in the same spot. He looked over at the leaves in the trees. He looked at the fertile ground, alive with new and old, wondrous and plain vegetation. His mind took him to his classroom at the school that he had attended. He remembered the teacher. He remembered the telling of the story of the story of Rabbi Akiva. His mind wandered, and he could picture himself sitting in the classroom and listening to the lesson. The story began with the telling of the Rabbi as a young man. He was a shepherd who was tending to his flock of sheep. He would sheer off their wool when the spring time arrived; he made sure that the sheep grazed, made certain that they bedded for the night; and he helped the mother lambs deliver their babies. While the sheep grazed he closed his eyes, and he would pretend that he was a great learned Rabbi. When he was not daydreaming, he would look over the pastures, the miles and miles of green grass. Sometimes the grass was high. Other times the grass was sheered to the ground, because the sheep had been grazing.

From a distance away, he would see a wolf coming down from a mountain steep. He would signal the sheep with his staff to go back into their pen. The wolf would growl and sometimes other wolves would join in the howling chorus, but the sheep were kept safe.

He would look forward to seeing the lovely young lady who would sit by his side for hours. They would talk about the distant creatures and animals. They would talk about the sheering of the sheep. They would talk about the heavens and the skis. They would talk about the big desert up ahead. They would talk about his becoming one of the greatest of Rabbis.

A wind started to blow and Sam awoke with a start. He would open his eyes and rub them. He would think at first, "Why are their no sheep?" Then he would sigh, "There are no sheep, because this is the woods in Nazi Czechoslovakia". He asked himself the question, "Are there any wolves lurking around?" He looked. With the sun shining brightly at the end of the day, he put his hand to his forehead to block the sun, and then he looked as far as he could for any movement any grey wolves or the real wolf, the Nazi wolves. He heard a bouncing sound, and he turned instantaneously, shuddering and feeling a sudden chill. His instincts told him to hide. He darted quickly behind the nearest bush and waited. It was not long before he saw a rabbit jump out of a nearby bush. "My", he said to himself, "I am jumpy today", and feeling his heart beat slowing down, he stood up and continued on his mission. He had walked for two hours and then sniffed smoke in the air. He walked slower and his eyes became the magnets for the discovery of the fire.

As the smell of the smoke got stronger, he spotted four logs where a fire was smoldering. He looked in amazement. As his eyes caught the glance of four cigarette buds that lay close by, he recognized a can that was burning in the smoldered fire. "Someone was here, maybe five hours ago", he guessed---maybe two, three people", as he looked carefully at the foot prints. He said, "It could have been anybody, but it might have been some German soldiers". He knew now that the Germans had been in the woods. He gripped his fingers tight into a fist.

He backed up his footsteps and tore a branch from one of the trees and swept away his footprints. As he stood tall upon the nearest ridge, he searched through the trees for the quickest way out of the woods. He emerged from the thickness and thicket of the forest trees and their camouflage; it was just before nightfall. The streets seemed quiet----no way near the teaming action, which was before the war; he sighed to himself as he visualized the people shopping at stores, children running home from school amongst the people who were walking; men making their way with pushcarts, which were loaded with wares, fruits and vegetables. No need for the symphony conductor to point out everyone's part in the performance: the streets were deserted. As he hurried to the jeweler's housed, he saw a lone man hurrying, darting like a sprinting rabbit, as he carried a long loaf of bread and a long, thick roll of salami.

"Well", Sam said, "I see one other Jew, who has eluded the Germans".

It was only a few more houses and then he would be at the jewelry shop. As he looked through the glass squares, which were etched in the thick wooden door, he could see an SS officer, who was buying a golden necklace---a ruby dangling from its center. Sam knew he had to hide in the bushes behind the building. He had seen the officer's motorcycle on the side of the house so he was certain that he could determine when it was safe to go into the jewelry shop. He munched on a piece of the bread his mother had packed for him.

The jeweler asked the officer, "Would you like me to wrap the necklace?" "No", the officer said, as he smiled, and he boasted, "I will carry it in my pants pocket like this and he put the box in his pocket. The officer took some money from his other pocket and flicking the bills deftly through the fingers of his hand, he counted out loud, "One hundred and fifty dollars". He slapped the money on the counter with a bang, and he said, "Good-bye, I will see you again".

The jeweler put the money in the cash register and thought, "They act so arrogant. If he knew that my wife was a Jew, he would grab her and the children, and take me to a camp too!" Just as he looked up, he had finished putting away other lockets and making the display case presentable, he caught a glimpse of Sam. He squinted his eyes and looked through his thick, metal-framed glasses as though he were checking over a gem with his eyeglass, saying, "Don't I know you? He moved his hands like he was conducting a symphony and acted as though his thinking power was in his hands. "Yes you are one of the Freier children", he said with an air of assurance.

Sam said, "Yes", in a quiet, watchful tone of voice and searchingly looked carefully at the kind, expressive eyes of the jeweler. He hesitated for a moment, cleared his throat so that he could speak clearly, and said, "My mother sent me to you. She said that I could trust you".

The jeweler whispered, "Sh, quiet" to Sam as he placed his index finger in the middle of his closed lips. He waited for a few minutes as he watched the minute hand move around the number 12 for five times and then he made sure the door was closed. He put the sign, closed, on the outside where the sign slid into a grove he had made. He turned the key in the lock and pulled out the key and put the key away in the middle draw of his desk.

He walked over to Sam and asked, "Why, what has happened?" The jeweler asked, "Are you all alone?" he asked with the sound of concern in his voice, and he waited patiently for Sam to explain.

"My brother, Martin, is very sick with a cold. My mother needs money for the medicine. She told me to sell the ring to you", and Sam's eyes looked puffy as he could not help but stare into the eyes of the jeweler, as if to say, "Please do not disappoint me", and he breathed in a large gulp of air. The jeweler had known the Freier family for many years and with an expression of concern on his face, he went over to Sam and asked, "Could I give you 250.00 German marks?"

Sam sighed with a sound of relief and was ready to jump up and down and said, "Yes", and he reached deep into his pocket for the ring his mother had given him. The diamond ring had receded and had burrowed itself into a corner of his jacket pocket, but was still there. Sam felt the ring and instinctively felt the diamond. Sam breathed puffed his breath quickly. Without even thinking, while blinking his eyes about ten times, he handed the ring over to the jeweler.

The jeweler clasped the ring in the folded fingers of his hand. With his eye glass attached firmly and pressing almost into his left eye, he looked into the channels and inner recesses of the colorful stone, which radiated rainbows. It was almost as though he was looking into a crystal ball and silently asking, "When will this awful war end?"

"Hum" he said, "This is a well-cut diamond. And he opened his left hand, and said, "I will have to give you $250.00 German marks more. The jeweler put the ring down on the counter and reached into his pants pocket and quickly took out a wad of cash. After counting the money, he gave Sam the money and said, "I am so sorry that you are having such a hard time". Sam nodded and then a blushing redness filled the colors of his cheeks, and the man thought that Sam was going to cry.

Sam went to open the door when the man called at him and speaking loudly, "Please, take some bread, and cookies, and some fresh pot cheese with you and remember that the ring will be waiting for you when you come back". Sam shook his head up and down once, and looked at the man through the lens of a tear on the front of his left eye, and said, "Thank you". His heart pounded away----beating to the tune of goodness. He was about to say, "If we make it back", and he could not mutter any other words, as his face turned red and more tears began to flow. Not wanting the jeweler to see him crying, he turned and walked out the door.

He knew his task was not completed. He had to find the doctor's office, and then he had to take the long trek home. He looked up into the sky and breathed more easily. He snapped the first two fingers of his right hand, "Remember, fear not, you will survive, because my father says that I will".

He stood outside the jewelry shop and looked carefully at all of the stores, which were lined-up across the street. He spotted a pharmacy. He looked to see if anyone was watching him for it was now almost instinctive.

There were people walking in the street. One or two were carrying breads in their hands. But they were hurrying along, and this gave him the confidence to walk amongst them. He pulled up the collar of his jacket as though he was cold and he walked boldly on. He walked into the pharmacy and stood behind a woman who was buying some cough medicines and cough drops. The lady thanked the pharmacist and Sam moved up front in her place. He pushed the souls of his shoes up, arched his nose high and looked even taller than he was. He blurted out. "I will have the same as the lady," and the pharmacist reached for the bottles, which were on the shelves behind the pharmacist. "By the way", Sam asked, "Is the doctor nearby?" "Is something very wrong?" the pharmacist asked, and he looked Sam over very carefully.

Sighing and thinking that perhaps he is questioning too much and is being too careful and that Sam looks like a regular fellow, he said, "The doctor lives just down the street in the big old white house with the white fence in the front of it". Sam nodded and left the pharmacy, while swinging the bag back and forth that was in his hand. He whistled as he walked and to anyone watching him, it would easily have appeared that he didn't have a care in the world.

They laughed some more. No one spoke about the war. No one spoke about tomorrow. Joseph said, "We are safe now". They fell asleep where they were sitting. In the town of Micholovce, the war waged on. Jews who had been hiding behind hidden walls were found. They were immediately deported by train to a concentration camp. The air around the town was gray and gloomy. The taste of ashes and burnt fire powder was on the tongues of the few Jews who were not caught. Desolation, depression, hunger oppressed those who were not caught. Many, like Joseph fled to the woods.

Joseph awoke to the sound of the water rushing in the nearby stream. He bathed and ate some more mushrooms and then went back to the others. "Anna", he said, "we must find a better place to hide". And he paused and caught his breath and felt the blood rushing through his arms and fists, "we must build a shelter that will not be found by the Germans. They began their march to safety through the uncharted territory. They walked on. They covered many miles. Sometimes there were trails, but other times, there were no trails. Joseph stayed close to the stream. Occasionally, they would see a group of grayling fish rising to the surface. Joseph took off his shirt and made it into a make-shift net and scooped up two of the grayling fish. Bernard, my brother and I cut up the fish pieces and we ate a delicious meal. We were most grateful.

It was almost nightfall, and everyone's feet were sore and ached. Stomachs growled for want of food. Lips begged for a drop of water, but Joseph told them to walk deeper in the woods. Night and its scary darkness were falling heavily upon us. Joseph held up his hand, and we knew we would finally stop for the time being. Everyone sighed with relief. Joseph said, "This is a clearing that I had visited just once before when I walked through the woods with my own father when I was a very young boy. We had gone on a hunting trip for deer and we had gone further than we had expected to go. It took us a while to find our way back, but we learned the landmarks, certain thicknesses in the woods, unexpected crevices, caves, but most of all to follow the stream, because the stream is always the source for your location and for food."

Sam called out, "look father", and he pointed to a tree, and then he pointed to another, and then to another, and then yet another. "You have found trees that grow quince." "Oh, yes, Joseph said, and there are wild berries that are you can eat too. They are just up around the bend". They all sat and rested. They picked the quince and put some away in their knapsacks. They rested, but Joseph insisted that Sam stand as the watchman.

My father's foreman brought us food whenever he was able. He came many times by horse and sleigh, looking like a perfectly innocent ride. No one would question him. He was to say that he was looking for pine cones for decorations on the Christmas trees and the front doors of houses. Or he was to say he was looking to see what animals were coming close to the town----to see if h could catch some deer------the Germans loved deer meat; venison was absolutely one of their favorites.

Once he brought us bags of onions. My mother mixed the mushrooms with the onions and we ate heartily. We got tired of eating the onions though. Once he brought us some Christmas cake with icing on it; it was a sight to behold; a breathtaking treasure worth more than gold in the middle of the woods. The taste of the sweet sugar lingered in our mouths and sweetened up our thoughts about these tragic times of having to hide in order to survive.

Aside from the daily survival of finding food, keeping warm and being safe, there was the problem of dealing with boredom and the constant fear that we had to contend with. Most of the time, we played chess with my father, and this sharpened our minds and we always discussed our moves, which helped us to develop our thinking and to get our minds focused on something else. We prayed together. We talked a lot about the Bible, its history and why the characters in the history were rewarded or punished accordingly. I always had my opinions and I always seemed to disagree with my father, but in the end we saw each other's viewpoint and we learned from each other. If we had had paper there, we could have written a commentary on the Bible, and it would have been a very informative one.

We talked over our problems, our fears about the Nazis, mostly; but my father tried to stir us away from this, because this promoted crying and depression. It did not help us. My father told us, "A lot of this is not under our control. A lot of this is not under the control of G-d either. G-d is omniscient, yes, but there are millions and millions of people and creatures in the world and G-d cannot be everywhere all the time. My father would always tell us, "Do good deeds. Read the Bible. Elevate yourself. Study to get ahead in life! This way you will signal the angels and they are the messengers who report directly to G-d.

CHAPTER 12

SAM'S ADVENTURE

One day, Sam was walking at a brisk pace in the woods. The trees in the dense forest bowed their graceful branches, as once in a while leaves would fall off gracefully, descending through the air in hoops and loops, and falling gently to the ground. The colors of the forest were a complete contrast to the gray, molding, decaying, and often bombed-out homes and businesses in Micholovce.

Sam breathed in the scent from the smell of the blowing of the multi-shaped, colored leaves, and flowing grasses; he whistled along with the chirping and whistling of the birds as they chattered and peeped out their calls. He smiled when he saw a flock of geese flying overhead.

But he quickly stopped smiling as he remembered the pictures in his mind about neighbors and family being rounded up and pushed into cattle cars. He shook his head and cried for a minute, and said to himself, "must go on, must go on in spite of the Germans", and he stepped up his pace. "It helps to pick up the pace. I think a lot less about the dangers," he paused. "Hmm, seems like just yesterday that my mother was looking over the stove and watching to see if the noodle pudding and baked chicken were warm enough. She would always make certain that the door to the stove closed tightly, and she would drape her dishtowel over the handle of the door of the stove". "Oh", he cried silently, "my family will never be the same".

Sam was on a mission to find food for his mother, and father, and sister, and three brothers. Every day was a new mission to stay alive. Every day was a new quest for survival and sanity. "Oops", he thought to himself, and he immediately turned around and looked behind himself, "got to remember to always be on guard", he muttered to himself. He chuckled, "maybe I look like one of the trees or maybe I am invisible to the Nazis…Wouldn't that be something—a real war weapon—invisibility". Moments passed and he got a grip on himself, saying with courage, "No such luck—have to face this". Sam stepped up his pace and walked briskly—even though thickets of entwining bushes lay ahead. He had been walking for over an hour, but Sam showed no sign of weakness. Sam was muscular with broad shoulders and taller than most of the men his age. His eyesight was very sharp and his mind was very keen. Suddenly and quickly as the wink of an eye, a brown colored hare with propped up ears darted out of the brush and thicket. It shilly-shallied back and forth for a few moments. Eyeing Sam for a flash of a second as his eyes rotated, he made a beeline dive for the thicket up ahead. Sam shook his head from left to right a few times—"missed out on a special dinner" he said to himself. His mouth watered for a plate of rabbit stew, cooked over an open fire in a big pot. "Might even have some berries and mushrooms on the plate to eat with the rabbit stew", he said, while slurping his tongue, as he pictured the meal in his thoughts. His family had never eaten rabbit before the war, but faced with the situation of starvation or eating animals that were not considered kosher, and found running wild in the woods, the family chose to eat whatever they could find.

Blessings were always whispered before and after meals and often Joseph talked of someday eating kosher foods. Sam often thought about the cholent, the potato puddings, rice puddings, chocolate-layered cakes, fresh baked apple strudel, baked sweet potatoes, and fresh roasted chickens. He could still smell the sweet aroma of the food. He could still taste the dill in the chicken soup. Sam often thought about his brothers. I was his favorite brother. This is my story about Sam. I am Martin.

He sang music like a Cantor. Sam sighed. Sam looked up into the sky. The sky seemed so high and yet reachable. He felt he could put his arm out and that his fingers could touch the sky. He stared or a few minutes at the sky---it was a wonder to him—the clearness, the smooth stretching out of the clouds in the sky---even a short smooth line of pink ran through one of the clouds----Sam was in awe of its beauty. His heart began to beat a normal rate.

Birds flew high in the sky this September morning, providing an assurance that it was safe to roam through the woods. Sam was cautious, however. He knew that he should look over the terrain, and leave a mark on one of the trees every mile or so. Then Joseph, his father could easily follow him. As he went along his way, kind of a zigzag path amongst the tall and sheltering pines, he felt his legs moving upwards as the slope got steeper and steeper; but the muscles in his long legs held him tightly so that he did not lose his balance. He, too, had been trained to listen for sounds----he knew the sounds of birds, the sounds of guns, the sound of motors, the sounds of snapping twigs---and he knew that any sounds had to be investigated and guarded against!

He stopped walking and listened. There were no sounds, except for a soft rushing sound. It was the sound that he could not identify at first that was unnerving. With a puzzled expression on his face, he walked a few more paces, then stopped, and listened very carefully. "Strange", he said to himself, and then he realized that the soft flowing sound that he heard was the sound of the ripples of water. He sniffed quickly into the air and decided that his nose, and not his ears, knew best—he would follow the scent of the water. The trail led to the East. He walked quickly, stopping only to engrave with his pen knife the letter "S" into the black, ruddy, ridges of the bark of one of the particularly taller trees: for that was his signal and signature, adamantly stating, "I am here"…"I dare you to take me"--- all in one combined thought: while the war waged, and when he had to fight for survival every minute of the day.

The smell of the fresh water became stronger and stronger; he smelled green algae that had reached the surface. He quickly searched with his large, rounded, light blue eyes------looking for the body of water he had come to believe was there. His tuned his ears in hopes of hearing even the smallest of sounds, and surveyed the area more carefully, saying, "in these deep woods, anything area can be easily hidden from view".

Birds flew swiftly overhead as they swooped and darted out from the straggling briars and the overgrown bushes that surrounded the lake. The fresh smell of green grasses, and wild flowers, and moist untouched earth permeated the air. Rustic looking crisp-shaped leaves remained suspended on the branches of the monumental sized trees, but there were signs in their color that they were looking forward to fall.

He smelled the rushing waters better now, as the scent permeated his nostrils and put his mind at peace, and assured him that he knew that he was doing; yet there was an ominous and foreboding silence about the deep woods, as he muttered to himself; "there is a secret here—I feel it in my bones, and I sense it with my whole being".

The birds chirped continuously to each other, as though talking about what was happening in the woods. The animals softly chattered all day and nervously ran about the terrain, hinting that they knew what the secret was all about". Sam looked on. He muttered to himself, "Watch carefully—these are the two words of survival".

He walked further about another 60 feet and passed through a thicket, getting his shirt torn at the wrist, while his pants were torn at the right knee by the thorns of the wild rose bushes that wanted him to stay and gnawed at him and looked as if they wanted to chew a piece off of him. These branches of the thicket had held fast and pulled and tugged, trying their best to stop him from passing; but he tugged and pulled with all of his might until the strong grip of the vines quickly knew who was superior and quickly released their tendon grip. The thicket, too, whispered quietly in the air—"**There is a secret**". Sam listened and thought, "I can almost hear the "shush sound echoing from tree to tree".

With a quick startle of a sound, a chipmunk rushed quickly out of the thicket. It darted to a group of trees towards the right. Following the path of the chipmunk, while squinting with his eyes, he saw it! Puffing hard with his lips, the lake unfolded slowly before his eyes, as it had done to its own world and its creatures so many times before in the forest.

Pristine light blue water extended as far as the keen eye could see. It was flowing downwards in a soft, slow, warm rhythm of its own----almost hypnotizing Sam, especially as the sun gently dotted its highlights of natural colors on the very crests of the waters. About ten feet above the large body of water, a small waterfall with a width of five feet, poured precious flowing water all day and all night long. "Fresh cold water to refresh my body and my soul", Sam thought and he supped up handfuls of the precious water. He suddenly heard the sound of a soft-sounding siren. He turned 180 degrees immediately towards the sound.

As the momentum of the water moved past, the second **secret, another secret** was revealed---- With stretched out arms, and feet almost welded together in a straight pose, a figure slowly appeared by the bank of the lake. She had long black hair dangling from the sides of her head, which flowed downward towards the narrow depths of the river. She was clothed in a long dark blue skirt and a long-sleeved white blouse.

The sun shined ever so brightly, but the water was chilled. The young woman floated with the movement and the rhythm of the water. Peacefully, she glided on the surface of the water, and she moved ever so slowly with the gentle waves to the edges of the water's banks. Her mouth was open as she was singing the same tune over and over again in a high-pitched tone. Sam could not figure out the name of the tune.

Seeing the young woman was a precious moment in time where Sam said to himself, "I can forget about the war for a few moments at least. But his caution about the Nazi hunters and his training took over, as he crouched behind some large bushes and surveyed the area. He thought to himself, as he blushed and felt for the yarmulka in his deep pocket in his pants. He asked the question, "What do I do now?" He was comforted by his education for the answer to his question---for as a Jew he knew that it was forbidden for a young man to touch a young maiden. He remained almost mute for at least a few minutes, watching her floating and drifting to the bank. He could not decide what to do. But as the water moved her to the shore, he knew that he had to make a decision. "Nothing stands still", he said to himself, and he said, "I will just talk with her".

She emerged from the water as a goddess who came from a castle from beneath the waters. Walking with straight and complete strides, without flinching or bending her knees, she held a 'pinch' of her blue skirt in her left hand. Continuing on, she walked to the magical, mystical, gigantic trees that inundated the mossy turf of the nearby woods. Sam blew a big breath and puffed another breath and said to himself, "Speak to her before she disappears!" and while stammering and clearing his throat, he rushed to the woods.

He waved his right hand in the air and shouted loudly, "hello there", forgetting about the Nazi hunters for a moment. The young woman stopped in her strides on top of the wild, gray, green, mossy turf. While her footprints imprinted a momentary mold on the ground, her head turned, giving her dark blue eyes a chance to aim a glance at him. She stood surrounded by the majestically graceful, burnt umber and green colored leaves of the outstretched branches of the trees. Drawn on her face was a duo-expression of fear and consternation. She called back with a grip on her voice, "Who are you?"

Sam blushed as he answered. "Hello there", as he put the fingers of his right hand in his mouth and bit down, his teeth grabbing at the nails of his fingers. The young woman took a step towards Sam and in a firm tone of voice, she called out, "do not take another step", and she stammered and said, "I am not alone". Sam responded by holding his hands high in the air. No movement from either of them for at least five minutes as they both stared at each other. But Sam broke the standstill, as he moved backwards one small step at a time. Sara breathed out heavily, calling to Sam, "who are you?" For a moment, Sam hesitated. He stared at her long dark black hair, and her slim, tall figure---all in one swoop. She stammered and looked like she was about to tap her left toe, and she asked, "Who are you?"

Sam collected his thoughts as though drinking, slurping them in, and said, "I am Samuel". He stuttered, "We are hiding from the Nazis in the woods". Pausing, he said in a calm tone of voice, "my family has a place two miles down----in the deep woods". She slanted her head a little bit to the left and asked, pointedly, "down where?" Sam pointed his right index finger to the South and said, "you see that tree just behind the clearing--- well beyond that the trees are so thick that you can never see a person"... "Well, if you were to go another mile, you would see some large logs piled up", and he cleared his throat, "we built a bunker under the logs".

"Oh", she answered in a softer and friendlier tone of voice, as she stepped a few steps forward and swiveled her hips to the right and then to the left. As she protruded her large dark brown eyes, she stared hard at Sam for a minute, and paused and asked in a questioning tone, "Why are you here?" Sam hesitated and looked at her for a moment, noticing that her clothes were wet, clinging to her body. He made believe that he did not notice, but his inner thoughts were dancing with delight, as he was noticing the beauty of her body.

His thoughts wandered to the girl that he had liked; Hannah lived in the big house next door. She had grown remarkably into a beautiful woman. He remembered that she had a different type of beauty for she looked like a china doll and was always tiny. She was always laughing and smiling. Often he was invited to join the family on Friday night for the celebration of the Sabbath. There was always the tastiest of home-made noodles, which was cooked in hot chicken soup.

There was always a blessed red wine that tasted special for it was always a combination of sweet and sour---it was special for the Friday night dinner; and he delighted in tasting the wine when a cup of the wine was passed to him. He remembered singing the song Shalom Aleichem with all of the people standing at the dining room table. Hannah's father led the singing for the Sabbath blessing with a heartfelt sense of reverence. Sam licked his lips as he remembered tasting a piece of the freshly baked spiritual bread.

A tear fell from the corner of his left eye, as he thought of the magnificent stone-built synagogue that he worshipped in. He remembered going up the 40 marble front steps, which slowly led him to the four magnificent, very large, heavy to hold the handle: doors; where even as a young boy, he felt a sense of awe and of being part of history and tradition.

Passing the stone-white, cement-molded figures of the two lions, which were kneeling on their knees, but were nevertheless propped up on the very front of the wide banisters on each side of the stairway; this was always a momentous moment. To him the lions stood for the tribe of Judah---a reminder, as the Rabbi had said, "Of our past glorious history and our hopes to return to our homeland in the future. The lions were awesome figures—ready to protect; appearing so real like they were ready to jump off the podium to attack anyone that threatened the synagogue; ready to claim their natural rights as kings. They were on guard with keen, questioning eyes through the day and the night, and yet their eyes sparkled with stars that radiated out into the open that sent the message, "We are here until the age of eternity."

At least one usher stood at the front of the magnificently, hand-carved, mahogany-colored doors to the front of the synagogue. The ushers were people from the neighborhood. Two of the ushers were over 6 feet tall; two of the ushers were short and stout; two of the ushers wore golden rings on their fingers. They all wore yarmulkas on their heads, easily identifying themselves as Jews---the common threads that bound them in life as friends. Each usher had the appearance of a pious man, with eyes exuding expressions of kindness that questioned automatically, "Are you all right"?

They were neutral in their acceptance of people, always unassuming about anyone who entered into the realm of spiritual destiny of the synagogue. Each usher smiled an automatic welcoming message of greeting, saying "good Sabbath" to anyone who walked through the arches of the doors. This was the way: following the tradition that had been handed down for centuries: from generation to generation.

The white, marble stone floor of the first hallway provided space for everyone to gather. The stoned floor echoed the sounds of the footsteps as the worshippers hung up their hats and coats and picked up their Bibles from the hand hewn and polished bookcases, whose shelves often sagged slightly from the weight of the books. The tall, hand hewn, hand stained and varnished, thick wooden doors to the sanctuary had large wooden handles, which helped grip the door for that final push when opening the door, which, of course, led to the kingdom for worship, somewhat to the freedom of the mind.

It was very common to see: men going in alone, women going in alone, men and women walking as a couple, fathers and mothers holding their children by their hands---they all walked into the sanctuary, each with a hope of connecting with God in the spiritual as well as the worldly way. Even the smallest child seemed to understand that a feeling of warmth and love was in the air and that this special spirit was undeniably part of G-d.

A massive golden covered ark, which housed six well-covered and hand-scribed in special ink torahs, was centered in the middle of the podium; it instantly drew your attention and made you think that you wanted to join others in prayer. You glanced at the people who were sitting in the high arched velvet padded chairs on the podium near the ark. They were chanting the prayers, and one started to think of the meaning of the prayers even before one found a seat and to settle in it.

In this room of spiritual reflection and remembrance, shining golden rays radiated toward the audience and toward the podium. Meaningful, memorable Hebrew words were cast on the outside casing of the podium. Inside the precious ark, the torah scrolls were covered with a rich-looking, plush red velvet material. Small dark blue, red, and green precisely cut, square-like stones of sapphires, and rubies, and emeralds adorned the outside of the plush covers of the torah scrolls. A magnificently crafted miniature silver depiction of the human hand, called in Hebrew, the yad, was hung on the shining wooden posts, one each at the sides of the torah scrolls.

The high arched walls of the sanctuary, which were decorated with squares of stained glass windows, provided anyone with a vivid imagination a chance to dream about treasures and far off exotic places. The walls in the sanctuary echoed the voice of the Cantor and the rhythm of the music was soothing to the soul of the worshippers, as they repeated his words and chanted their portions of the Bible.

Going downwards from the sanctuary was a narrow stairway that looped around the corner of the wall and descended almost straight down; it was carpeted with a thick pile, almost an inch of woven, deep-red velvet wool. The stairway led to three large size rooms downstairs: one was a chapel, ornately decorated around the Rabbi's podium with large golden letters, which translated Hillel's message, "do onto others as you would want others to do onto you."

The other two rooms were classrooms. One classroom was used as a social hall for the Saturday afternoon kiddush luncheon. A hot cholent, a special dish almost like a very thick soup was always served, which consisted of baked beans, boiled eggs, and boiled potatoes. Chocolate cakes, and sugar cookies were always served. Sometimes a lavish luncheon was provided for the entire congregation in which lox and white fish, and different salads, and cakes were served.

At the end of the hall was the fourth room; it was the main kitchen for the temple. It housed two large stoves, which were made out of cast iron and which were kept on all night and day so that the food was always served hot; two wooden iceboxes; and a very large sink, which had two cubicles and both had faucets with a slow but steady leak.

Sam shuddered for minute as he collected his thoughts. A bird flew above him and called to his mate, "Caw, caw, caw". The sound of the bird reverberated in his ears; he soon realized he had been deep in thought. He said to himself, "I remember when the Nazis came to take Hannah and her family away", and his thoughts were solemn, as he recited a silent prayer. He felt that he could not talk about Hannah. His thoughts were interrupted when Sarah blurted out, "well, answer me!" and she held her hands tightly on the top of her hips, almost pressing into the muscle that covered her hipbone.

"Oh, yes," he stammered, and his face reddened, and the heel of his right foot tapped up and down automatically, as if his sub conscience were in control of his thoughts. Sarah looked at him, staring mostly at his large, very round-shaped gray-green eyes; she stood on her toes like a ballerina, for she must have been at least a foot shorter than him. He walked closer to her and then stopped after going a few feet. He stammered and said, "I am sorry for not answering you." She took a half of a step backwards and smiled politely as she asked, "then you must be a Jew?" He had not spoken of his Judaism to anyone in a long time, and he stuttered the words, as he answered, "Yes, yes, I am a Jew", as though he could not swallow the words any longer, but yet the words were medicine, which consciously, when whispered the message, he felt better. He paused and then asked Sarah the same question, with a serious expression on his face, "Are you a Jew?" She looked for a moment as though she had been caught off guard. She stammered and then said in a meek voice at first, "yes", and then she held up her head and said the words much louder, "yes, I am a Jew". They both paused. They both looked at each other. Sam smiled and started to laugh. She smiled back at him and then she laughed.

She paused and then said, "Well, I should be getting back to our hideout". "Stay for a little while longer", he prompted her, and he tapped his foot lightly on the sandy soil of the ground while waiting for her to respond with the answer. She put her hands down to her sides and smiled, and said in a polite tone of voice, "I must really be getting home". "Well, all right then", he said with a sad tone to his voice. She turned, and she walked down a trail that was laden with stepped-on overgrown grasses. He watched her walk off and looked to see if anyone else was in the woods.

When she had almost gotten out of sight, he said to himself, "oh, I forgot to ask her name", and he shook his head. After pausing, he stared at the point in the woods where he could only see the trees, he said, "I will see her again".

He began walking along the pathway to the hideout. "This place is really beautiful", he said. "The air is so fresh. Birds are flying freely, free, free all the way in the sky. I can hear them sing as they fly overhead and far, far in the sky". Little red apples grew on apple trees, making the apple tree look alive with tiny red bells and ready to sound their music, or fall down off the tree; and offer their tiny, delicate bodies for nourishment. Little pears grew on quince trees, tasty with a lasting combination of tartness and sweetness that lasts for a while in your mouth. Bushes and bushes of small black berries surrounded the pathways around the lake. Birds of all sizes and colors, one of which is called the black stork fly over the waters of the lake and look for small fish to feed on. Some birds feed on the berries.

On the far left side of the lake, was a small waterfall, which flowed over the rocks and over the edge of the mountain. The water of the lake was pure, pristine light blue. Small schools of trout-like fish, the grayling fish swam about two feet below the tranquil, mild currents of the water. When caught, they always put up a good fight. It was always unexpected. They seemed so tranquil. Very large sized mushrooms with pointed tops darted up in circular clusters near the edges of the lake. They lived for about a week and then disappeared as suddenly as they had appeared. Then new clusters of mushrooms appeared elsewhere, dotting the earth here and there.

"This is like the 'Garden of Eden'", he said to himself, "or could I be dreaming?" He thought, "I have to touch one of these apples to feel it to believe that it is real". He reached for an apple, and plucked it off. Then he pulled off two others. Munching and savoring the taste of each morsel, he ate one of the apples. He wiped his mouth with his cloth handkerchief and put the handkerchief back in his pocket. He felt happy. He started to sing a song, which his brother Martin had written just about a year ago. He walked down a hill, which had tall grasses growing along its sides, singing the song softly, while shaking his head to the tune of the music. He was enjoying himself.

He stopped at one of the bushes and pulled off a handful of red berries;

he put them into his right pocket. He walked quickly and putting his hands to his sides, he felt he had grown taller.

He started to think about the sweet taste of the apple; he reached into his pocket for another. After eating the apple, he reached into his pocket and pulled out some of the berries. He sucked on the juice and swallowed the berries, sometimes throwing them up in the air and then snapping down hard on his teeth when he caught one or two in his mouth.

It was growing dark when he reached the outside of the hideout. Looking around and listening very carefully for any strange noises, he reached into his pocket and took out his watch and looked at the time. "My goodness, is it that late?" he muttered to himself. He crawled under the pile of large logs and knocked once on the entrance. He waited for the reply. In a few minutes, there was a knock on the other side of the rock and with his hands held tight, he pressed hard on one of the logs and moved the rock away and crawled through the opening.

Remembering to close the opening of the hideout, as his feet touched the ground, he pulled at the log at tugged at the log until it sat firmly on the entrance hole. Slowly, he walked down the ramp until he reached the first underground room. "Sam always muttered to himself, "at least we are not living like in the dark ages", when he entered the room in the cave. The cave was clean and Joseph had done his best to build some attractive, wooden furniture.

The smile on Sam's face told the story that he had met someone. He walked into the middle chamber, where the family usually sat on the wooden long, drawn-out couch that Joseph had constructed with the boys and was ready to tell his story. "Sam, where have you been?" Joseph blurted out with a sigh of relief in his voice. "Pop", I was exploring a part of the woods that we have never seen before", he answered.

"Well, next time let me know ahead of time. I worry. I think always about the Nazis", Joseph said, with a sense of concern in his voice. "Yes, Pop, I know that they are always around us. I can assure you that I was always careful", Sam said. "Well, then" Joseph said, as he nodded his head with a sense of pride and pleasure, "you have listened and learned well". "Thanks Pop", Sam said, and he smiled and sat down on his chair, which was constructed for one person, but the chair had a high back frame. They sat for a few minutes. Sam yawned. Then Joseph yawned. Joseph went into the next room to his bed to sleep. Sam followed.

Joseph's devoted friend, his foreman, had secretly carried the blankets and coats in a wagon late one evening. When the foreman's horse would not go into the deep woods, he himself made a stretcher from wood and he put the coats and blankets on the top of it, and pulled it along until he came to the hideout. The family had used the blankets and coats for warmth and always blessed Joseph's foreman for them.

Sam was tired from the long walk home, and he could not sleep. His thoughts were about the beautiful, lovely, 'maiden' that he had met in the woods. He laughed, as he muttered to himself, "I do not even know her name", and he fiddled with his mind, guessing to himself, saying, "is it Sarah, could the name be Miriam?" He put his hand across his mouth and muttered, "I hope that she is real". He yawned and turned over on his side, but he still could not sleep. He started to think about the bombed out house of their neighbor who lived next to them in Micholovce. He began to sweat and breathe heavily. He wondered if his home was still standing. He knew he had to get up and walk around; otherwise, he was going to throw up. He climbed out of the bunker. He stayed outside the bunker, but near to the entrance. He could see flashes of light pointing in scattered directions in the distance. He lay on the ground and pounded the ground with his fists. Tears flowed from his eyes in a steady stream, making it hard for him to see, but he knew where he was. He puffed out some breath quickly and said to himself, "good to be safe from those monsters".

A creature darted out from behind the rock that was behind him. "Oh, let it live", he said to himself instinctively. He stood up and wiped the tears from his cheeks with his bare hands. He said to himself, "If a small creature like that can scamper around and want to live, then why not me?" And then he felt an inner sense of peace from all of the torment. He sighed. He let go of his thoughts and fell asleep. He lay for hours on the ground.

The sun rose and shined through the tall branches of the surrounding trees. Sam was dazed when he woke up. He closed his eyes and questioned his surroundings at first, but then remembered that he had gone out of the bunker. His clothes were soaked with sweat. "Well", he said to himself, "this will not do", and he walked to the nearby stream. He waded into the water and shivered from the cold. His thoughts came back to the bombing that he had seen from a long distance away the night before, and he reflected about the large room that he had had to himself in his house. He wondered if his house was still standing. He wondered if he would ever see his home again. Keeping his head above the water, he immersed himself into the water. With his arms he pushed the ripples of water away as he kicked his feet with all of his strength. When he grew tired and hungry, he came out of the water. He said to himself, "I know better than to stay out all night". He reflected about the young woman that he had met in the woods, and he smiled. He asked himself the question, "Do you think that you will see her again?" He cried out the answer, "Yes, yes, I will", and he went to the hideout.

Anna was bending over, frying mushrooms for breakfast on the underground, indoor oven, which stood about a few inches from the ground. Sam asked, "Mom, you are okay", and she smiled and looked up at him with admiration. He sat down and slurped the small, torn pieces of mixed raw and cooked mushrooms into his mouth, hardly chewing them, and drank some hot cocoa, "thinking this cocoa is good even if it does not have sugar. When he had finished eating his food and drinking his cocoa, he felt better and announced to Anna, "I am going to look for berries and mushrooms". She looked up at him with admiration. She hesitated for a minute, only because she wanted him to stay a bit longer, but then she said, "Okay son"; and she continued to stir her fruit mixture of wild berries and quince for the next meal.

The sons of Joseph Freier came with a look of determination and strength and resolve on their faces---they were united in their cause to survive; they knew that they were being hunted because they were Jews. They knew that they might never return to their magnificent home. They survived and later were reunited with their father and mother and sister, Edith. My father's foreman helped us a lot. Without him, and the people that he knows, and the papers that were issued, and my father's money, we would not be alive today!

Martin remembered the walks he took in the woods with his grandfather. He remembered riding on the wagon with Grandpa David. He could hear his grandfather's voice ringing out, "hudya, hudya", and Martin could see his grandfather in his mind as though it was just yesterday, as his grandfather, dressed in strong, thick cotton cloth pants and a warm flannel shirt, and a warm three-quarters leather jacket loosened the reins and let the two horses speed up. He asked himself the question, "how could all of this have changed in one night?" He bit his lips. He almost cried, but he stopped himself.

Sam opened the door slowly and slipped into the foyer and waited. He breathed heavily from the excitement even with his mouth closed. He circled the living room. A voice called out to him. "Sam, Sam, is that you?" Sam turned toward the couch and saw his father. "Dad, I did not know if you were alive", he exclaimed, and he rushed towards his father and hugged him. They hugged each other until they were both out of breath.

"Sometimes I wonder if I am alive", his father said slowly and sighed with a sad expression on his face. Joseph paused and then with both hands extended asked the question, "and what of your brothers?" And he looked down on the ground and shook his head.

Sam blurted out, "they are alive and waiting outside". Joseph rushed to the door and opened the door with both arms outstretched. "They ran to each other----father and sons. They held hands. They sobbed. They cried for joy. They danced. They danced round and round. They danced the Harrah. Tired and breathing heavy, Joseph quickly looked around outside and motioned for the boys to come in. Anna came into the room. They looked at her and said, "Glad you made it mom." Martin's eyes met hers. They understood each other's feelings. Martin wanted to cry out of sorrow; the next minute he wanted to cry out of joy. Anna wanted to hold her son in her arms, but she dare not think of love and family. No. No. Not in these times. These times demanded strength and strength alone.

She said to herself, "what about the next time", and she was silent as he walked in to the kitchen, and as the other boys followed. Joseph shook his head back and forth. He said, "It is a wonder that we are all alive". Anna squeezed her eyes and then opened them widely and said, "The Lord has given us life when so many others are dying at the hands of the Germans. But, Joseph, your cunning has saved us so many times". The boys nodded their heads.

"What are we doing about food?" questioned Sam. Joseph cleared his throat and said, "Well, at the moment, we are living on what we buried". "Well, there are seven of us now and the food will soon be gone", Sam stated. "Yes, you are right to be thinking of food", said Joseph, "and I will speak with Andrew about working at the factory, and I was thinking of going over to the baker to see if Dubi has any bread". "Well, okay, do you want me to go with you, dad", Martin asked. "Stay here, it is a short distance and I will be back before you know it I promise" Martin smiled and Henry smiled.

"But what will we do with ourselves?" cautioned Edith, as she leaned on the right heal of her foot and held her hands on her waistline". Anna finished the question, "you can clean the house with me or you can read one of the books we have managed to hide". Edith snorted, but kept quiet, because she did not wish to upset her relationship with her mother.

Joseph waited for his turn to talk and then interjected, "the boys can cut wood with me". He looked at the boys for their approval and saw sour expressions on their faces. Knowing this, he said, we can always play a game of chess and he saw each of the boys smile. He knew that he had to find the chess boards, and he did.

Joseph knew what to do. He scratched with his nails at the wallpaper and made a small hole. He reached in far to the right of the paper, underneath and in back of the wallpaper; he felt with his right hand for some dollar bills. When he had grabbed a handful, he covered up the hole with a tiny piece of wallpaper. He pocketed the cash and said to Anna, "I will be back in an hour". He walked to the main square of the town. It was not far for his house for they lived just on the outskirts of town. He went into the bake shop, after finding a small sign on the outside door, which said, open; and he walked in and he waited.

He waited and paced up and down, while he wiped the sweat off of his brow. A young man who could not have been more than 15 came from the back apartment 5 minutes later. Joseph cleared his throat and asked, "is Dubi in?' The young man squinted his eyes and hesitated and then said, "Why do you wish to see Dubi?" Joseph replied, "I wish to feed my family bread, and cheese, and cookies". "Well, have you brought money", Dubi has asked me to ask everyone, and he sighed, "we just cannot give everything to everyone or we would not have anything for ourselves". He paused and then Dubi himself came out from the back room and said, "hello Joseph", nodded his head, made sure that his spiritual cap was correctly placed on his head and said, "if the Germans find out that I am hiding food, they will cut off our heads".

Joseph backed away a few feet. He sighed and then asked in a polite tone of voice, "How much food can you spare?" Dubi said, "Well, for you Joseph I can spare a bag of breads, and muffins, and cookies, how is that?" Joseph smiled at Dubi and felt excitement in his heart.

Joseph put his hand in his pocket and put the waddle of paper money into Dubi's hand. "Here", he said. "Will this be enough?" Asher counted the money. "It is more than enough". "Wait here," he said and I will bring out some breads and cookies". Joseph asked, "Can you spare any eggs?" "All right, all right", he said, while shaking both hands in the air. He left. He went into the back of the store.

Every minute of waiting for Joseph seemed like an eternity. Finally, the tall, broad shouldered baker and friend that Joseph had known for so long came out from the back room with a woolen bag filled with the breads and other bakery goods, and said, "Here, Joseph, this is yours". And he paused and said, "Everything that you paid for is there". Joseph looked at the tray with eyes wide open. Joseph took some of the smaller breads

78

and hid them in the inner pockets of his jacket. He took two muffins and hid them inside his hat. He hid a bag of cookies in his jacket pockets. He looked in all directions while standing on the top of the front steps of the small house, which was set somewhat back from the street, and he walked fast like a wolf hound who knows exactly where his next meal is coming from and he is going after it.

He walked with her slowly down the hills and paths to her hideout. Thoughts flashed into his mind about how he would walk with his family every Sabbath to the synagogue. Images of the synagogue flashed through his mind. With his memory he followed his images of the synagogue and walked up the steps to the large ascending doors and entered once again the world of spiritualism, the world of spiritualism which he was born into. The sound of the cantor singing could be heard louder and louder as he walked closer to the sanctuary. He wondered if he would be able to find the page where everyone was reading, without asking his father. In his mind, he visualized, he sat proudly with his three brothers and father amongst all of the men and sons. He chuckled as he remembered, "the big discussion at the house was what the meaning of the Rabbi's sermon was". When he left the synagogue after services, he always walked slowly as though weighed down by all of the new thoughts mixed with some of the old thoughts that he already knew.

The smell of the blossoming flowers and roses, and the beauty, particularly, of the black roses in the spring and in the fall would always sweeten the scent of the air in Czechoslovakia. The rose is the symbol of love. The rose petal scent blended with the oily smell of the surrounding pines. The sight of the majestic holly shrubs with shining, thumb-shaped red balls, with sharp, green, pointed leaves was imprinted in his mind. Forgetting his step, and tripping on a misshaped branch that had fallen from the tree, the sound of the snap caught his attention, taking his thoughts away from the peaceful times, and placing the times to the present----the here and now---- with the Nazis strong arm.

Sam walked along the winding paths through the woods. He was thinking of the man he had seen lying on the ground. He muttered to himself, "the man was a beggar." And he bit down on his lip, while thinking, "wonder how he will survive this war".

Sam found the entrance to the hideout without any sightings or unusual snappy sounds. "Unreal," he muttered to himself as he fell into a deep sleep.

Sam had agreed to meet Sarah once a week. It would be a Sabbath to look forward to. Another six months of the war had gone by. It was August and the weather was very hot for the month.

The next morning, Sam said to his mother, "I must go fishing today", and he trekked through the woods, fully clothed with a warm jacket and pants. Anna questioned herself, "why would he go on such a hot day?" She called Martin and said, "see if you can follow your brother" and as she hesitated, she said, "in case he needs you". Martin followed him and did not lose him even though he stayed far behind Sam.

Sam headed straight to the lake. The wind blew on his back and he said, "Wind, blow at me some more, and he ran faster, while looking for Sarah from a short distance. Sarah was sitting beyond the clearing. Puffing, his cheeks almost red like a red-colored apple, he walked up to her and said, "How are you?" She turned her head and said, "I am okay" in a soft, sad-sounding voice. They sat for a while. She gave him three left over sugar cookies; and while biting on one, he put the others in his jacket pocket and patted the outside of the pocket in an automatic response.

He fished and she sat next to him and together they watched the string at the end of the pole. She saw the water move in circles with the circles floating farther away from the center circle. As she watched, she began to see glimpses of her life---living in her home---running up and down the twenty-five steps on the stairway, inviting her friends over to do their homework together, going together as a family every Saturday to the temple, coming home from the temple and having a discussion on the part of the Bible that the Rabbi discussed. Her thoughts were interrupted as Sam suddenly called out, "wow, this is a big fish. He tugged at the line and tried to pull it in. Sarah watched, her eyes bulging, as she jumped up and down in excitement. She had never fished before. The thought of fishing for a meal and getting a fish to eat pleased her.

At a hill along the way, which was well hidden from the pathway that had been formed by people trekking through the same area, Martin watched. He smiled and looked in amazement and thought, "my brother Sam has found a girlfriend----and of all places---in the middle of the woods. Contented that he had solved the riddle of where Sam went all these times in the woods, he headed home to the hideout, on guard always for Nazis or collaborators.

His mother greeted him with a swelled excitement, saying, "So what happened, so what happened?" Martin blurted out with one quick breath, "Sam has found a girlfriend". "No?" Anna questioned. "Yes," Martin answered, and Anna stepped backwards and sat down on one of the wooden living room chairs and took out a cloth handkerchief and blew her nose, and for a while she sat and stared into space. Martin brushed against her side, and he felt her warmth, and he said, "It will be all right." She looked up at him, and she nodded, "yes", but there were tears in her eyes.

Not far from the lake, and close to some large boulders; and a few yards away from their hideout in the woods; Sarah's sister had begun taking sunbaths outside of the hideout. She had fashioned foil paper around a large piece of cardboard, and while she sat in a wooden chair, she held the cardboard under her chin. She closed her eyes, and she supped in the warmth of the sun. Sarah's sister had forgotten that a horrible war was raging.

The sun's reflection bounced from the cardboard to the nearby boulders, then up into the ridges of the mountains. The reflection bounced off from one rock to another. Per chance, the sun's rays announced the family's presence, signaling telegraphically, "We am here."

Unknown to most people, the Nazis were looking over the terrain, because of fear of an imminent confrontation with the Russian soldiers from the East. On that afternoon, a group of Nazi soldiers were on patrol on the top of the mountain. As they descended the mountain, one of the soldiers spotted the reflection of the sun shining on one of the boulders.

"What is that?" He yelled out loudly as he pointed to the reflection. His lieutenant quickly peered through his binoculars. He said in a bitter-sounding voice, "Cannot see exactly where it is coming from, but we must find out from where!" He yelled to his men, "Could be a signal from a Russian or a partisan, or a Yid!" He quickly ordered everyone to search. He led the way, with his hand nesting on an open holster.

The clouds had grown gray and Molly, noticing that the weather had changed, she thought, "Must be going home." She folded the sun board, and brushed off her clothes. As she walked, she stopped to pick wild purple flowers, and she thought; "I will bring these home for my mother."

A shot from a shotgun whizzed out. It pierced her head. Stunned, she stood still, shaking--her body getting colder. The soldiers ran down the pathway so quickly, crushing tiny white flowers with the weight of their big, ferocious boots. Nine tall, green-clad soldiers surrounded her, each soldier aiming his rifle at her head.

"Where are you from?" the German lieutenant shouted. She stood and stared at the soldiers, not believing what she saw. Cold and shaking, her lips changed to a shade of purple. "Where are you from?" the lieutenant shouted again and before she could muster up the strength to answer, he walked up to her and slapped her in the face. His impatience grew and he slapped her two more times.

She fell to the ground. Her hand accidentally brushed against his rifle. Acting only on animal instinct, one of the soldiers fired his gun at her. She lay on the ground where she fell, lifeless.

"Why did you do that?" the lieutenant shouted at the soldier. The soldier stood at attention and answered, "These Jews are not that smart". The lieutenant stared at the soldier and then laughed. He shouted, "We will find their hideout. Macht schnell", as his eyes automatically surveyed the surrounding area and left.

The German soldiers followed the pathway, walking on the fallen grasses and leaves. The wooden house, squelched between tall, thick pine trees, slowly was discovered through the spaces in-between the leaves. The sharp eyes of one of the German soldiers spotted it. The soldiers banged down the wooden door on the front of the house. Their rifle butts loosening and instantly boring gores and chips into the skilled craftsmanship of the door; unable to resist the force, door crashed to the floor, revealing, Sarah's mother and father. Two shivering figures hovered together and the fear written on their eyes spoke more than words could ever say.

The lieutenant shouted to his men, "let us finish this disgusting job today. Shoot them!" Two lifeless figures fell. Cold on the creaking wooden planks of the kitchen floor, they remained an imprint in time, testifying to the German soldiers' vulgarity.

From the distance, Sarah and Sam heard the rifle shots, at first dazed by the meaning of the shots. Sam grasped the reality a few minutes later. He grabbed Sarah by the hand and held her tightly. "Do not go," he yelled, while his head moved in every direction, trying to sense if the Germans were coming near them. She struggled with him, pulling her hand away, until she broke from his grip. She cried out, "I must go to my family," while tears clouded her eyes.

"You must be quiet and you must hide", he quickly responded in an almost harsh tone of voice, and he grabbed her by the arm. She tugged with him for several minutes and pushed him away. She ran to her family. He called to her, "come back" with frightening thoughts palpating in his heart. She ran swiftly and was soon out of sight.

Sam stopped in his tracks, knowing the dangers. After a few minutes, he bowed down his head. Thoughts rushing through his mind, he knew, nevertheless, to follow his instincts. He ran to hide under a bramble bush.

Through the thickness of entangled vines, he heard the sound of three shots—identifying death. He cried like a baby---stopping only when his breathing had became belabored.

Nighttime fell with a deep chill, and he knew that the darkness would give him a better chance for escape. His mind turned to prayers---reciting what he could remember of the evening prayers. He dried his tears and was about to stand up when he heard the sound of leaves cracking, and the "woof, woof" sound of a dog.

Shaking with fright, he crawled deeper into the bramble bush, his posture in a fetal position. Torn by the thorns of the brush, he suddenly remembered that if he crushed the berries, his scent would be gone; he quickly rubbed the berries into the fabric of his clothes. He rubbed the crushed berries on his hair.

The ominous sound of the crackling leaves got louder. A dog barked. "Is it one dog or two dogs?" Sam asked himself. He shuddered and prayed, saying the words, "help me God," over and over. The sound of the dog's bark came closer to the bramble bush. Determining that it was only one dog, he sighed with relief. The dog sniffed in the air and stopped for a second and then he charged with front legs leaping forward----catching the scent of a white, brown-spotted rabbit.

The soldiers, running quickly, jutted up and down, the flaps of fat on their midriffs bouncing with a rhythm, up and down and then again. In no time the tune of their boots changed pace to almost a stop, as they were tugged down by the pull of the muddy surface—the hands of the 'dead' reaching and stretching to pull them into the ground with the help of the wind.

Sam never looked back. He had only a little more to go when the back of his legs throbbed with aching pain. He felt alone in a conquered wilderness, silhouetted by the disappearing moon, a glow in the dark, the only light. Bending his head while rubbing the back of his legs, thoughts rushing to his mind like, "could he have saved her", threw him down to his knees. He cried out for his friend, Sara. He cried out, "I have grown to love her". His heart was raced. He lay prostrate, attached to the ground. An owl perched high up in one of the surrounding trees, began to hoot. The opera continued through the night.

Martin had heard the quick, piercing sound of the gunshots---shooting arrows-----flying high in the distant wind, whizzing by. They were like arrows from the warring tribes of the Bible. Peering through spaces between branches on a pine tree, he spotted Sam. He walked slowly through the unshorn, tall grasses, hearing the opera of the night.

Sam was lying prostrate, his form crushing the tall grasses beneath him. Martin reached for Sam's arm and helped him get up. Sam began to cry. "Save your tears brother, until we are safe", Martin cautioned him. Sam, out of anger, pushed Martin away. They struggled for a few minutes, and Sam fell, saying, "I have nothing to live for", and he covered his face with his hands. The night grew even darker as Martin tugged at Sam's arm and helped him get up. Martin prompted him, "Come on. Come on brother. Let us get out of here!"

Sam grunted and walked at a slow pace. "Let me be", Sam called out. Martin answered firmly, "No. Never give in to the Nazis". "They are everywhere", Sam said as he leaned his head backwards. Martin, squeezed his eyes shut, stepped backwards a few paces and he held his lips tightly together. He said firmly a soft tone of voice, "Hashem will deal with the Nazis. You will see! You must have faith."

"Oh, will they, he laughed loudly. Saliva collected in his mouth and he bent forward and spit out. He watched the spit water seeping in the ground. He saw a flash of light. Faces started to come forward. Whole bodies walked out of the muddy earth. The bare bodies gathered and huddled together, men and women and children; they danced, holding outstretched hands and they turned round and round and round. Stopping for a minute, they swayed from side to side and then clapped their hands and tapped their feet to the melody of the music that was in their minds.

Smoke appeared, coming from small pipes that were installed in the ground. Slowly, the smoke inched up to the tops of their heads and then covered them. In a moment, the music that was in their minds stopped, and they were all falling to the ground. Sam's vision blurred so he could not see where the bodies were.

Sam closed his eyes, afraid to open them. Martin shook him, as Sam's head and shoulders went back and forth, and then back and forth again, and he cried, "Come on, come on. Wake up brother." Sam opened his eyes, and he blurted, " I just do not know why they were all killed by the Nazis". While lifting up his arms, he called out, "help me God. Help me brother". Tears fell from Martin's eyes, as he gulped, barely able to mutter the words, "yes". He bent down and reached for Sam's hands.

Sam staggered as Martin walked by his side. The distance to their bunker home was not far, but it seemed like an eternity. Martin broke the silence, as he spotted the opening of the underground bunker. "It is tragic, but you must go on." And he said firmly, "But you must go on, because you are a Jew". Choked up with tears, Sam muttered, "yes, I am a Jew", and then, shuddering, he held his head down and wept bitterly. Sam cried out, "She was a Jew, too!" Sam, his legs weakened, and his knees throbbing, beckoned Martin, "Can we sit a little bit?" Martin shook his head for a moment, clearly expressing "No". "You know the story. The longer we sit and talk, the longer we set ourselves up as targets". Sam nodded his head up and down in approval and said, with a murmur in the tone of his voice, "she was so young. She was so beautiful". He sobbed, "I loved her. Brother, I loved her." Martin answered him, as he crouched down and sat on the sandy ground, "you must remember that you are a Jew and that there is a purpose for you on this earth. You will remember her."

"Oh, a purpose?" Sam asked with an agitated tone in his voice. "Yes, God is always with us even though it seems like he has abandoned us", Martin told him. Sam got up to his feet and questioned, "tell me, what did Sarah ever do that was wrong?" Martin spoke in a firm tone of voice, "God is good and God is merciful…. The Germans killed Sarah and her family and the Germans are certainly not Jews". Sam smiled a small smirk, as he said, "no, I guess not, and then he said, in a more serious tone of voice, "They are Germans, devils". "Yes, they are, and our God has quite a job on his hands saving his people from the throes of the devil," Martin answered. The brothers walked on, side-by-side.

After at least a half hour had gone by, Martin paused and said, in a calm tone of voice said, "his messengers just cannot be everywhere in the same time". Sam was calmer now, but was exhausted and said, "okay, but I think I need to rest". Martin replied quickly, "Come with me, my brother and let us live; let us escape to our hideout, and let us live to see the day when the devil is completely subdued by God and his angels. Sam muttered, "I say Amen to that", and Martin put his hand on the top of Sam's shoulder, and they walked together towards the hideout. Sam was almost like an inanimate stick, propelled by a physical force of motion at first. Then thoughts raced to Sam's mind about Sarah. He called out, "Martin, she could have become my wife. She could have borne my children. We could have walked together to the temple; she could have sat on the other side of the curtain."

"Yes, that is true", Martin said, as he wondered if Sam was able to go any further. "We will rest for a minute, and we will talk, but only for a minute," he cautioned Sam. Martin thought and then spoke, "I cannot answer your question, even though I agree with your thoughts". He paused and then he said, "Think--- back to the beginning of our history-- that has been handed down from generation to generation---Jacob entered the 'promised land' after much strife." "What does that all mean?" Sam questioned, as he looked up to Martin. "It means that there are bad people and that there are good people and this is the way that it has been for centuries", Martin said. "Do you think that the curse will end?" Sam questioned. Martin looked up to the stars and paused for a moment, and he sighed, "I think that God wants the hatred to stop, but has not figured out how to make people want to love. Of one thing I am certain---God chose us as his chosen people. We are a people whom are loved by God." He paused and then smiled as he said with a comforting sound in his voice, "I know that one day there will be peace", and Martin cried softly to himself. Martin blew his nose and wiped the tears from his eyes with his cotton handkerchief and announced, "hopefully the forces of good will subdue the forces of evil soon", and he paused and then said, "I would like to sing, maybe even be a cantor, and maybe even write a book". Sam asked, "but what would you write a book on?" "Oh, that is simple," he paused and nodded his head in affirmation of his thoughts, "why I would write a book about us brothers and our mother and father and sister". Sam asked, "Would it be about the war?" Martin answered, "Oh, yes".

Sam chuckled as he said, "I would like to be a jeweler". I would like to see the glitter and glow of gems." "Well, there you have the idea—we will live through this horrible war if we keep our wits together. We will survive. Let us go now brother, please," Martin said to Sam.

They had the hideout in sight, when Sam faltered and fell to the ground. Martin coaxed him, "come on brother, like mom always says, 'the camps, the camps'. Sam we got to live, we have to fight for survival, because otherwise we will end up in the concentration camp, the camps."

"Will we ever live a life without fear?" Sam asked, as he closed his eyes for a minute. Martin answered, "You and I have to hope".

Sam said, "Martin, sing something to me." "You got to be kidding—in the middle of the woods with Germans creeping and crawling around, no thanks," Martin puffed the words out of his mouth.

Sam stopped cold and cried, "Brother, I need you to sing the song about the Messiah coming". Martin paused and pursed his lips and said, "I will sing it softly", and he chanted the words, "the Messiah is coming. We will all be free". He sang the words over and over again.

Thoughts rushed through Sam's mind, however, and he cried, while shaking his hands in the air, "I have to go back to bury them. I just have to". "Hold on, brother, we are here to be together, to survive together", Martin said with kindness and understanding with a soft expression and concern in his voice. "I must go back, I must go back", Sam protested.

"You will go back when we tell you it is safe to go back, and you will not go alone!" Martin said in an adamant tone of voice, and he asked, "Do you understand that?" Sam continued to cry. He would not move.

Martin said, "Stay here and don't move". Martin ran to the hideout and tapped the signal, five taps on the opening. Joseph heard the signal, and he tapped one time back. Martin went back to Sam and waited with him. He knew that his father would find them soon. Sam gave in to his weary body and fell asleep. Martin sat down beside him and waited.

After a short while, Martin heard a strange rustling noise through the grasses; he looked up and spotted his father walking around them. He knew to wait quietly. Shortly, Joseph appeared in front of them suddenly, at first like a shadow in the back of a dark curtain. His finger was pointing to his mouth, and Martin shook his head, and nodded "Yes". Joseph and Martin grabbed Sam by the arm and walked with him; they pulled him down into the hideout. Martin sighed a large sigh of relief, when he bolted down the hideout door.

Sam slumped to the floor, despondent, his face colored ruddy red. He lied for two days, hardly moving his body; it was his own form of hibernation from life. On the third day, he opened his eyes; he looked around the room as though in a daze, and cried out, "I am hungry." Everyone stood by his side and smiled at him.

Anna brought him a wooden bowl filled with broth, which she had made from the roots of nearby plants and had cooked a wild bird in it. She made sure that Sam sipped it all as she sat with him.

Joseph told her, "Bernard, and Martin, and I will find the bodies and bury them when it is safe". He paused, and shook his head, trying to overcome the sadness.

Sam muttered in his sleep, "I loved her, I loved her". The rain came in torrents the next night, and Joseph said to Bernard and Sam, "the Nazis will not be roaming through the woods in the height of the storm. Besides," he pointed out, "Martin will be the watchman while Bernard and I dig the graves". "Won't the ground be rather hard in late October?" Anna queried, while she sat arched in her chair. Her eyes glazed with fright as her eyes opened wider. Joseph answered her, "I think the rain will protect us and will soften the ground". And he paused and then said, "anyway, we don't expect to be there very long!"

They exited the hideout one by one, each waiting a few minutes until they were sure they were not being watched. They walked separately, with a good distance between themselves. They had rehearsed the way so that they knew exactly where they were going, in case one of them got lost. They had a signal, the sound of a bird cawing, if they spotted any trouble, and they knew to lie down and hide.

It was not until two hours later that the three men came upon the fallen bodies. The bodies appeared lifelike, lying in the rain with their swollen eyes wide open. The blood from their wounds had washed away in the rain. Joseph and his sons knew their task was gruesome, but it had to be done. Joseph used a large branch like a shovel and he started digging one large grave for the family. Martin positioned himself on the top of a nearby ledge and crouched down. Bernard stood next to his father and watched as the earth was slowly moved and the grave opened into a wide, deep pit. Joseph was nearly done when he felt something metal-like under his shovel. He said to Bernard, "You dig now and find out what is buried here!" Bernard dug around the metal object and then went into the large crevice and wiped the dust off of a large metal box. Bernard lifted the metal box by himself and placed it on the ground on the top of the crevice.

The box had rusted slightly on each of the side corners, but it stood solid. Bernard spoke with a sense of anticipation, "I wonder what is in this box?" Joseph replied with excitement rushing through his veins, "Well, open up the box and let us find out!" A gush of air rushed at them as the lid was quickly removed. They peered in and both expressed a sense of 'awe' at the same time, "why, it is cans of food and jars of cookies, and there is some money!" Bernard smiled and looked at Joseph and asked, "what should we do?" "I will tell you in one sentence" Joseph responded with a tone of decision and said, "Leave the box where it is, while we will bury the family".

When the ground was covered with a top layer of crumbled earth, and they had finished the prayers that they were able to remember, Joseph made the sound that was the signal. Martin knew to come over quickly. "Look, it is a shame to leave this food. The food will only rot or the Germans will find it and have a feast on it" Joseph said, and he continued, "stuff your pockets, stuff your bandanas. Hide the tin box, and let us get out of this place!"

They ran at first from the scene of death, never looking back. When they had reached the woods, they slowed down the pace and walked single file. The trail had guided them along their way through circuitous, but parallel perimeters, inundated with overgrown brush. All three carried somber expressions on their faces. Their eyes, dazed with fright, were aimed straight and sometimes looked up to the sky for guidance.

They were more aware than ever that they were alive. Silently, they renewed their prayers to survive and to be free. Almost home, Joseph muttered to himself, "tragic waste of life". He collected his thoughts and squatted with an arched back, as he said to his sons, "I want you to tell Sam that we buried the family in the best way we could".

Bernard asked, "Should we tell about the food that we found?" "Tell no one nothing. Tell no one!" Joseph said in an adamant voice. His sons bowed their heads simultaneously and replied, softly, "yes". They reached the entrance of the hideout, but lingered for a while in the nearby woods. When they were certain that they had not been followed, they descended into the safety of the bowels of the ark.

Anna swept her feet across the hardened ground, crying, as she said in a garbled, anxious voice, and she held out her hands, "come and have some hot chocolate." All three men nodded their heads in an upward motion, and they sat down with somber expressions on their faces at the wooden kitchen table.

A new day began after a restless night. Just before the rising of the dawn, blasts of cannon roared their fierce, explosive force in the distance. Joseph, and Martin, and Bernard awoke with a shudder. Sam rolled over in his bed, snoring, adding to the noise of the cannons.

Anna started to cry. Edith sat on the ground next to her mother—not even an inch separated her body from Anna's, as Anna held her tightly. Joseph sat in his chair, staring at the opening of the cave. They all stayed where they were for at least two hours.

Through a crevice in the wall, a rat nervously ran out of its hiding place and ran nervously towards them. Edith screamed. Joseph and Martin ran around the room after it, cornering it as it neared the opening. Martin stepped on the rat with a fierce stomp, and the rat was silenced.

Joseph climbed up the short distance to the opening. He opened up the hatch and threw the dead rat in the distance. Pink lines in the sky caught his eyes and gray-colored blasting smoke filled his nostrils. The sound of the blasts was deafening and frightening, making his body shake. The sound of bombs bursting, and rifles shooting, and the echo sounds of the wounded made Joseph say to himself, "no good, the war must be closer than I thought," and he closed the hatch door and came down the ladder.

Joseph said to his family, "pick up whatever you can. We must leave this hideout. We must leave now", and he started to pack whatever food he could find.   There was no discussion about what was going on. Everyone knew that they must follow what Joseph said. With heads bowed down, and expressionless faces, and with eyes half-closed, they each packed whatever food there was and rolled it in their knapsacks, which were hand-sewn from discarded jackets and pants. Not much time passed when Joseph demanded, "let us go!" and they all followed behind him. One by one they emerged from the opening in the earth, as though the dead had risen from their coffins. When they were all standing firmly on the outside, Martin mentioned to Joseph in a soft tone of voice, "pop, lift up the cover of the hatch and take out the Bible". Instinctively Joseph nodded his head in affirmation and pulled out the Bible, saying "I will carry the Bible in my knapsack. Certainly do not want the Germans to find it".

They kneeled down for silent prayer and Joseph quickly pointed to some black-barked colored trees, which were standing guard five yards away and they headed that way. They, the five men and the two women blended into the forest, as though they were shadows of trees moving with the wind. Fallen leaves lie rustling with the wind and crackled from the weight of their footsteps. Owls peered at them with rotating corneas from high up in the trees. Squirrels paused from their staccato paces and with arched-up hind legs, paused to look at them; rabbits paused to shake their puffy cottontails as they continued on their trek for some foliage in October. Mice scampered at a faster pace under the rustling leaves, nervously running towards a camouflaged hole, which was well hidden by underbrush. Chipmunks stopped to peer at them with anxious rotating dark black eyes; they waved their little furry tails as they dodged quickly over a rotted fallen tree and scurried along to their hideout hole.

The seven of them forged on, forgetting hunger, forgetting thirst, but remembering that dawn turns into dusk. After over eight hours of trekking through the circuitous prophetic trees, and up steep hills and rocks, and deep ravines, Joseph whispered through his many puffs of breath, "Look over there". Their eyes followed the pathway of his pointing right finger. They saw an opening in a cave. Joseph breathed in and out easier as he said in a soft-tone of voice, "this will be our new home", and they all followed him into the entrance of the cave. Sam was the last to go in. Martin held him by his hand and nudged him to come in.

The cave was dark, alluding to the fact that it was nighttime. They lay down their shattered belongings. One by one they fell down and lay on the cold damp floor, oblivious to outside world's cruelties and in a deep sleep. They emerged from their hibernation slowly the next morning. Light had opened up the day and had filtered through the opening of the cave. Instinctively they opened up their knapsacks and munched on their kernels of raw corn, and sour berries, and dried-out morsels of bread. They shared one jug of water. Sam did not speak. He stared at the wall of he cave most of the day. Martin coughed at times.

Light quickly turned to darkness. In the dusk, a deafening, resounding sound rang out. More shots of sounds rang out. Bombs exploded, instantly shattering trees in their path. Bursts of fire shooting out in demonic arches colored the fallen trees with tepid red and yellow colors. Smoke rose from the ground and obscured the vision of the naturally scenic distance. "My God," Joseph cried out, "the war has come to our old hideout".

And in the months that followed, Joseph led his family to find foods and water; he built with his sons a hidden entrance to the cave; he set up a stove in the back of the cave and camouflaged the exit hole for the smoke. Anna resumed the day-to-day life of survival, helping as much as she could with washing clothes, cleaning, and preparing food, and talking with her family. She cried silently for the dead she had known. Sam no longer ventured out into the woods alone. He spoke very little. He stared at the walls of the caves for long periods of time.

On one sunny March morning, Henry came running up the hill and sounded the birdcall, and they all listened for more warnings. As he ran, he panted for breath, his feet hardly making it up the end of the hill. Joseph ran to meet him. Joseph held his son by his shoulders and asked, "Who is coming?" Henry breathed in a large breath and then said, a hunter is coming!" in an excited tone of voice. "Run, quickly, and hide", he said to Henry. Joseph walked away from the hill and came from behind the hunter. Joseph called to the hunter, "you, there, hello", in a friendly voice. The hunter turned around and said in a surprised tone of voice, "I did not know that anyone else was living in these parts. "Well," Joseph replied, "just like you, I like the woods". "Oh," said the hunter and he took a deep puff from his self-rolled cigarette, and he laughed as the cigarette burned out while he held it in his hand. "Nobody could survive that bombing." He sighed, "Some of the dead are still laying there". "I am sorry to hear that", Joseph said in a kind tone of voice". "Well, I am on my way to the town, which is yonder", said the hunter. "Have a safe trip", Joseph said to the hunter.

Waiting to see that the hunter was no longer in sight, he headed for the cave. "The news is that there are dead German soldiers lying on the ground". Sam looked up, and said, "Maybe we will survive this war yet", and he went for a walk in the woods.

........fill in.

Then just as suddenly as it had begun, the silence of the guns told the story of the ending of the war. Thankfully, it was not the ending of the world and not the ending of our people. We waited for two weeks. It was already April; it was time for the Passover celebration. My father climbed out of our underground bunker. He stood up and stretched his legs and back. He moved his hands outwards and inwards as though he was talking with an angel, in his own way pleading that the war really be over. There were moments when I felt that we were the only people left alive in all of Czechoslovakia.

Joseph said, "We must prepare for the Sabbath". Sam replied, "Yes, Pop, it helps to think about prayers". "Yes, always remember that God is with you", Joseph said with a sense of honor, "and tomorrow we will hunt in the woods for food." We will look for mushrooms and berries that Anna can grind and then she can make a bread".

Joseph said with all of his strength, "come let us pray together". They had one prayer book for all of them. Sam smiled for he knew to say, "Pop, when we get back to Micholovce, we shall dig up the Bibles and prayer books that we buried in the back yard." Joseph smiled, and he said with strong conviction, "let us pray". Joseph held the prayer book. Together they sounded like one voice---a family together with one melody. They were a family together before the war. Their religion and faith in God was the thread that tied them together. Now it was the war and the Nazi horror machine that bound them together. Martin sang with his family. When he sang, his voice was so powerful that the walls echoed all through the cave's chambers; and out through the hidden smoke channel, dissipating with the winds and blowing from one stone to another, and never stopping until the sound reached the sky.

When they were finished singing, they looked at each other and nodded their heads in approval. They all hugged Martin. Joseph thought to himself, "it feels like the spirit of Judaism; this reminds me of the kiddush on Friday nights---taking the small sips of wine from the finest bottles of wine and passing a little of the wine to everyone at the table: the togetherness, the spirit of Judaism amongst us". He paused and sighed and squinted his eyes, and thought, "How the fresh baked bread tasted after we took that first bite before talking and before eating the meal. This is the spirit of life that we used to have before the Nazis with their tall boots marched into our towns; before they threw us wantonly into the lime pits, before they took us in crowded trains to the gas chambers; before our children lay dead on the streets from starvation". Joseph's hands began to shake and he gritted his teeth. Martin saw that his father was upset and asked him, "Pop, do you need me?" Joseph cleared his throat, and he said, "son, you know what I was thinking about". Martin said in a soft voice, "I know". Joseph left the room.

Joseph lay in the bed that he had hewn out of wood and had stuffed with tall grasses. The bedroom was big enough for a large bed and was in the back of the cave. In the cold months of the winter, he and Anna covered themselves at nighttime with the bear rug that a hunter had given them. It was warm in the chamber most of the time for the kitchen was attached to the bedroom. Martin, Sam, and the others slept in the other bedroom that was on the other side of the kitchen.

Old and dark green colored pine trees surrounded the top of the bunker for miles. The cones from the trees oozed with seeds---food for the family to store when the grounds were covered with many inches of snow and ice. The smoke from the kitchen stove blended in with the mists that always surrounded the tall and very old pine trees. The top of the kitchen vent was concealed by a screen, which was made from twigs. Joseph had built three large beds for his children so that they could sleep above the hard ground. Sam slept in the same bed with Martin; Henry slept in the same bed with Bernard. Edith had a bed to herself. They covered themselves with old quilts, which were made from old coats.

Joseph's devoted friend, his foreman, had secretly carried the blankets and coats in a wagon late one evening. When the foreman's horse would not go into the deep woods, he himself made a stretcher from wood and he put the coats and blankets on the top of it, and pulled it along until he came to the hideout.

Sam was tired from the long walk home, and he could not sleep. His thoughts were about the beautiful 'maiden' that he had met in the woods. He laughed, as he muttered to himself, "I do not even know her name", and he fiddled with his mind, guessing to himself, saying, "is it Sarah, could the name be Miriam?" He put his hand across his mouth and muttered, "I hope that she is real". He yawned and turned over on his side, but he still could not sleep. He started to think about the bombed out house of their neighbor who lived next to them in Micholovce. He began to sweat and breathe heavily. He knew he had to get up and walk around; otherwise, he was going to throw up. He stayed outside the bunker, but near to the entrance. He could see flashes of light going in scattered directions in the distance. He lay on the ground and pounded the ground with his fists. Tears flowed from his eyes in a steady stream, making it hard for him to see, but he knew where he was. He puffed out some breath quickly and said to himself, "good to be safe from those monsters".

A creature darted out from behind the rock that was behind him. "Oh, let it live", he said to himself instinctively. He stood up and wiped the tears from his cheeks with his bare hands. He said to himself, "if a small creature like that can scamper around and want to live, then why can't I?" And then he felt an inner sense of peace from all of the torment. He sighed. He let go of his thoughts and fell asleep.

The sun rose and shined through the tall branches of the surrounding trees. Sam was dazed when he woke up. He squinted his eyes and questioned his surroundings at first, but then remembered that he had gone out of the bunker. His clothes were soaked with sweat. "Well", he said to himself, "this will not do", and he walked to the nearby stream. He waded into the water and shivered from the cold. His thoughts came back to the bombing that he had seen the night before and he reflected about the large room that he had had to himself in his house. He wondered if his house was still standing. He wondered if he would ever see his home again. Keeping his head above the water, he immersed himself into the water. With his arms he pushed the ripples of water away as he kicked his feet with all of his strength. When he grew tired and hungry, he came out of the water. He said to himself, "I know better than to stay out all night". He reflected about the young woman that he had met in the woods, and he smiled. He asked himself the question, "do you think that I will see her again?" He cried out the answer, "yes, yes, I will", and he went to the hideout.

Anna was in the kitchen. She was busy frying mushrooms for breakfast. He said, "mom, you are okay", and she smiled and looked up at him with admiration. He sat down and slurped the mushrooms into his mouth and drank some hot cocoa, "thinking this cocoa is good even if it does not have sugar. When he had finished eating his food and drinking his cocoa, he felt better and announced to Anna, "I am going to look for berries and mushrooms". She looked up at him with admiration. She hesitated for a minute and said, "okay son", and she continued to stir her fruit mixture for the next meal.

Sam headed for the lake. He walked briskly, but he stopped to look and listen for anything that might mean danger. He thought about the shrubs and tall trees that encompassed the lake. As he went his way, he laughed as he thought, "Just uphill to get there and downhill to come back---that is the secret".

A raccoon with tiny little hands, whose belly bulged, and whose eyes had a natural black mask, darted out in front of him. Her young ones followed. They chattered softly and moved their little legs in an awkward way, as they struggled to keep up with their mother. Sam called after them, "come back let me see you again".

A mist hovered over the trunks and branches of the trees, making it hard to see, but Sam knew his way. "There are always clusters of trees", he muttered to himself, and he remembered what Joseph had taught him, "walk closely to the trees". He felt like a shadow---traveling amongst the trees, moving cautiously and in step with all the creatures, who knew that the woods were their only habitat.

A thorn from a wild rose bush gnawed at his right shoe's shoelace, and pulled at the lace, and untied it. He bent down to tie it and when he looked up, he saw her---in the distance, reigning supreme amongst the creatures of the woods. His excitement was beating the blood into his heart at a fast pace; he felt hot, but did not take off his coat.

The weather was still a little damp, but the ground was warmed by the bright sunshine of a late October day. His thoughts were composed mainly about 'her'. He asked himself the question, "should I rush over to her?" Then he realized that it was best to play hard to get. He thought quickly, "have to have a reason for being here", and he knew that his answer was the cluster of dead trees by the side of the lake. "I will say that I came here for the firewood", he said as he wobbled his head in affirmation. He bent down and started to gather the twigs, but could not gather two many, because the larger branches stuck to the smaller ones.

He broke off a few of the taller branches. "All right", he said, "trees die too". He began to deftly put together a raft with the wood, putting the branches together and tying them with strong weeds for twine; in his mind he visualized the raft as a magical raft, which could take him and his family far out to sea to an Island where there was prayer all day---and everyone could practice his religion, and where there was not the day-to-day searching for food. His thoughts were interrupted---for she came over to him.

Trying not to notice her, he continued to tear off the branches of the trees. She moved closer to him. He backed up from where he was standing, while tugging with a branch that was hard to tear off. He turned around quickly and said to her, "I almost fell on you". She looked at him for a brief moment and said, "I just wanted to say hello". He smiled and chuckled. He said, "Okay, hello to you too". She smiled. He bent down and picked up some of the branches. She hesitated and stood watching, but after a few minutes, she bent down to pick up some twigs. He said, "thank you. That is very nice of you to help me".

"Well, I guess your family will be warm with the firewood", she said. Sam replied, " Yes, this will help them a lot". He put the branches in a single pile, forgetting about making a raft. She threw some more dead twigs onto the pile. Sweat poured from Sam's brow. He wiped his forehead with the corner of his jacket. Squatting and bending his knees quickly to the front of him, he sat down on the cold, damp, fertile ground. She stood by his side as though she were a shadow. He coaxed her, saying, "sit down", and she did. She stared for a minute at his face and then smiled. He said to her, "I have a story to tell you". She sat demurely and answered, "yes". He hesitated and stuttered, and practically spit out the first word, "my father has kept us alive". He hesitated and then said, "He has taught us to escape from the Nazis at whatever the cost". His lips tightened on him as an autonomous function of the body.

"Where are you from?" she asked. He replied, stuttering, "I am from Micholovce". "Oh, that is a nice place, and do you attend school there?" "Well, I did until the Nazis banned us from attending school", he answered.

He, calming down, and breathing in and out, asked her, "What have you been doing with yourself?" She answered with a princess-like demeanor, almost doing an arabesque with her hands, and arms, and legs. With an assured tone in her voice, "I have a private nanny who tutors me".

"So you do!" the words sprung out spontaneously. He shook his head and said, "I am sorry, I should not have asked you that question". She shrugged her shoulders. She cleared her voice, while she held her nose a little bit in the air, and said, "it doesn't matter to me what you think about rich people".

His thoughts scattered all over. First to his own home, which was a mansion; he remembered the large size of his own bedroom; He gripped his thoughts and remembered something that Martin had once told him, "We must show humility to God, no matter what", and he felt a sense of assurance returning to his thoughts. He cleared his throat and said, "Well, I am not picking on rich people".

She smiled and asked the question, "have you ever been rich?" He shrugged his shoulders and looked at her and he spoke in a very soft tone of voice, "I have forgotten to think about money". He looked down at the ground and then at the sky.

She came closer to him. She looked at him for a minute with questioning eyes. She spoke in a soft tone of voice, "it has been hard for the last five years. He looked up at her and smiled and she smiled back.

The both of them breathed in and out, and Sam cautioned her, my brother Martin always tells me when I feel like I am going to despair that, "We must remember in our hearts that we are Jews". She nodded her head as if to say, "yes", while tears came to her eyes. Sam stared at the sky. She stared at the same direction in the sky.

The color of the sky was light blue. There was not a cloud to be seen. No airplanes flying overhead. Miles of trees could be seen. No trucks driving up to houses. No soldiers, marching, could be seen. Sam commented, "this place is 'peaceful; an oasis in the middle of a desert of oppression and depression". She nodded with her head in affirmation, while she pressed her lips tightly together. Her blue eyes shined with rays of sympathy.

Many moments passed. She broke the silence by asking, "what do you think you will do after the war?" Sam hesitated, and almost cried--- his thoughts jumbled, he said, "it may never end". He cleared his throat, saying, "I just do not know".

"Well, I am going back to my house", she said with an attitude of confidence. He looked at her, questioningly, and in a soft tone of voice, said, "You never think that maybe your house will not be standing?" She quipped, "no, never" and made a grunting sound. He looked at her with amazement. She answered firmly in a loud voice: "the house will be standing".

Realizing that she was in denial, he said, "Well, all right then". "I was thinking", he said, as he snapped a branch off from a tree, and then paused.

She coaxed him to answer her, in a questioning tone, "What were you thinking?" "I was thinking of becoming a jeweler," he said with a smile. "That sounds good to me", she said with her arms folded across her chest.

The color of the sky changed from blue to gray. The clouds were assembling. "Well, I must be going home", he said to her. She twisted her hips slightly and said, "You can stay for a while longer can't you?" "Well, I guess for a little while," and he paused and said, "looks like it is going to rain. I think I would like to get home before the down pour". "She waved her right hand in the front of her face and said, "Don't worry about it. You can always come to my hideout". He looked at her and smiled, and he asked, "are you sure that you have enough room?" "Of course we do", she answered most assuredly. The cloudiness faded just as suddenly as it had appeared. Like magic, the brightness of the sun shined brightly.

"How about we walk around the lake?" he asked her. Pausing, he said, "how about I ask you what your name is?" She looked at his eyes, her eyes glowing in the sunshine, and said softly, "Sarah". He smiled. Together they walked as they left their footprints in the sand----four feet with the same rhythm, beat of the music. He looked at the ripples in the water. She picked off the tops of the long grass.

He was thinking, "wouldn't I like to hold her hand", and he thought further, "her hand looks so delicate and gentle that it must be cold". He concluded to himself, "she needs a strong man", and he sighed, "I am just the one".

She was thinking, "with his pointed nose, and dark, wavy brown hair, and milk white skin, and blue eyes, he looks more handsome than a German", and she shook her head a few times up and down in affirmation. She looked at him and she frolicked in her thoughts, "he is so tall and handsome". "Hmm", I wonder what his name is", she said to herself.

They walked to the other side of the lake and then rested a few feet away from the edge. They looked at the lake as they continued their walk. "What is your name?" she asked as she moved her head sideways. "Oh", he stammered, "my name is Samuel", and he pronounced his name with a voice of distinction. She smiled and nodded her approval.

Stopping where there was a clearing of the wild grasses, spouting up and extending their tinsel apexes towards the sky, Sam bent down and cupped his left hand. Bringing the clear, pristine water to his mouth, he quickly supped up some water. He breathed in and out and wiped his mouth, saying, "this is really good, fresh-tasting water".

He saw her reflection in the water, flowing, flowing gently away with the ripples of the water of the lake. "Don't disappear on me", he said quietly to himself, and he got up and wiped his mouth.

Together, they gazed at the sky and stared quietly into the open and expansive space; both of them wishing for a peace and an end to the war. She spotted a shining, bright star and said, "I wish that I could reach up and pull down that star". Sam was amused at the thought, and laughed out loud.

She broke the silence by saying, "what are you going to eat for supper?" He hesitated, because his thoughts were not on food. He answered her, "most likely some of the mushroom bread we had last night". She exclaimed, "never heard of that kind of bread". "Well, we have had to be resourceful", he answered her with a chocking sound in his voice. She paused and then asked, "Do you have anything to put on the bread?" "Oh, yes", we eat the bread with some of the quince preservatives my mother has made", he answered, thinking of all of the hard work that went into it. "Your mom must be a really good cook," she said. Sam smiled as a response.

The blue skies gave way to a deepening gray color. Thunder roared like a lion and lightening bolted like the sky was angry: all of these were a harbinger of an approaching storm. The rain fell in a downpour. Sam's jacket got wet in minutes. Sarah's sweater was wet too. "Well, we had better get under some trees for cover", Sam declared. Sam spotted a cluster of old trees. "Come on with me over here", he called to Sarah. She followed and he covered her head and shoulders with his jacket, and they sat under the large trees together. They watched the rain falling. All of the leaves near them soon were covered with droplets of water. Occasionally, a rabbit would dart out of one of the nearby bushes.

They laughed a little. Sam said, "I am hungry". Sarah said, "You must come to my hideout and eat with us.

Sam hesitated, "well, all right, but only if you have enough food". Sarah quickly answered, "I know that we have enough food".

"But how do you really know that?" Sam asked her with a concerned expression in his voice. "I know because once a month we get a delivery of canned food. We bury the cans and use them when we need them", she told him.

"Would you have any fresh bread?" Sam thought out loud and asked, but then caught his thoughts.

Sarah answered with a smile on her face, "Yes. We do. It is rye bread. Do you like rye bread Sam?" she asked.

He answered without any doubt, as he was licking his lips, "Oh, yes. I love it". He paused for a moment, with his eyes protruding, and said, "I used to eat it all of the time with fresh butter".

The sun came out of hiding behind one of the puffy clouds and it succeeded in growing bigger and moving away from the disappearing cloud. The rain stopped as suddenly as it began. There was the smell of fresh green leaves in the air. The fresh smell of the leaves and the thought of eating fresh, baked rye bread put expressions of joy on their faces.

They walked slowly side by side for a while. Sam stopped suddenly in his tracks. Sarah hesitated and then asked him, "Why are you stopping?" He replied curtly, "in case you do not know it—there is a war all around us".

She hesitated as though she was dazed, and then she looked into his eyes, and she said, "Oh, okay". "You must remember!" he cautioned her.

She walked first and then he followed, as she led him into a ravine. Then up an ascending hill and when they reached a cluster of bushes, she said, "we are almost there". Sam cautioned her, as he held his finger on his closed lips, and she just stared at him, barely expressing any thoughts.

"You must not talk, and you must walk very softly," he cautioned, while whispering. She pointed to a direction in the air, saying, "Over there, see where there is the cluster of pine trees on the hill?" He looked for a few minutes, sharpening his right eye to project like a telescope and said slowly, "yes". She continued, "Well, there is underbrush in the midst of the trees and our house is in the midst of the underbrush". "That sounds fantastic. Wow, what a place to hide". They walked for a bit.

"Okay, then lead me to your hideout", Sam said, as he broke the silence. They walked up the steep hill and walked through and passed the dozens and dozens of thickly set pine trees, almost tripping on the large pine cones that had fallen recently; and there it was: thick brush and in its very midst a large wooden house. With hand hewn shutters, which covered its windows, and noticeable thick planks, deftly glued together for its front door, and it was untouched by the animals in the forest or the severe winters in the forest; the house stood still in time quietly, quite majestic.

CHAPTER 13

SAM GOES BACK TO THE WOODS TO SEE HIS QUEEN

Sam headed for the lake for the thought of 'her' propelled him. He walked briskly, but he stopped to look and listen for anything that might mean danger. He began to think about the shrubs and tall trees that surrounded the lake. As he went along on his way, he laughed as he thought, "Just go uphill to get there and downhill to come back---that is the way". And he started to hum softly to himself as he walked along the trail.

A raccoon with tiny little hands, whose belly bulged, and whose eyes had a natural black mask, darted out in front of him. Her young ones followed. They chattered softly and moved their little legs in an awkward way, as they struggled to keep up with their mother. Sam called after them, "come back let me see you again".

A mist hovered over the well grown trunks and drooping branches of the trees, making it hard to see and he was not sure what he was stepping on; but Sam knew his way. "There are always clusters of trees", he muttered to himself, and he remembered what Joseph had taught him, "walk close to the stream", but if the stream is not there, then "walk closely to the trees" and find a path or mark a path so that you can always find the way back". He felt like he was a shadow---traveling amongst the trees, moving cautiously and in step with all the creatures----wild, unknown, mystical, and whatever was out there; who knew, but that creature might have thought that Sam was encroaching in the woods on his only territory.

A thorn from a wild rose bush suddenly jumped up, almost like a wild dog attacking, but not as fierce; it gnawed at his right shoe's shoelace, and pulled at the lace, and untied it and then it pulled at the tongue of the shoe. He tugged several times, hoping that he would not have to leave the shoe, but finally the thick thorns gave way and receded back to their bush; Sam bent down, retied the shoe, and when he happened to look up, he saw her, the object of his affection---in the distance, reigning supreme, like a queen, walking with soft toes gently on the ground, amongst the small crawling and jumping creatures of the woods.

The weather was still a little damp, but the ground was warmed by the late afternoon, bright sunshine late in the day. His thoughts were composed mainly about 'her', her majestic appearance. He thought to himself that he had found the lady of his life, but she was also a depiction of a queen from long, long ago. She might have looked just like the Queen of Sheba. Oh, he was so happy with himself. He asked himself the question, "should I rush over to her?" Then he realized that it was best to play hard to get. He thought quickly, "have to have a reason for being here", and he knew that his answer was the cluster of dead trees by the side of the lake. "I will say that I came here for the firewood", he said as he wobbled his head in affirmation. He bent down and started to gather the twigs, but could not gather two many, because the larger branches stuck to the smaller ones.

He broke off a few of the taller branches. "All right", he said, "trees die too". He began to deftly put together a raft with the wood, putting the branches together and tying them with strong weeds for twine; and in his mind he visualized the raft as a magical raft, which could take him and his family far out to sea to an island where there was prayer all day---and everyone could practice his religion, and where there was not the day-to-day searching for food. His thoughts were interrupted---for she, herself, in the flesh, with her graceful stance came over to him.

Trying not to notice her, he continued to tear off the branches of the trees. She moved closer to him. He backed up from where he was standing, while tugging with a branch that was hard to tear off. He turned around quickly and said to her, "I almost fell on you". She looked at him for a brief moment and said, "I just wanted to say hello". He smiled and chuckled. He said, "Okay, hello to you too". She smiled. He bent down and picked up some of the branches. She hesitated and stood watching, but after a few minutes, she bent down to pick up some twigs. He said, "thank you. That is very nice of you to help me".

"Well, I guess your family will be warm with the firewood", she said. Sam replied, "Yes, this will help them a lot". He put the branches in a single pile, forgetting about making a raft. She threw some more dead twigs onto the pile. Sweat poured from Sam's brow. He wiped his forehead with the corner of his jacket. Squatting and bending his knees quickly bent in the front of him as he sat down on the cold, damp, fertile ground. She stood by his side, but very slowly and delicately. He had coaxed her, saying, "sit down", and she did. She stared for a minute at his face and then smiled. He said to her, "I have a story to tell you". She sat with a demure expression on her face and answered, "Yes". He hesitated and stuttered, and practically spilled out the first word and then it became easier for him to talk to her, "my father has kept us alive". He hesitated, and then said, "He has taught us to escape from the Nazis at whatever the cost". His lips tightened on him as an autonomous function of the body.

"Where are you from?" she asked. He replied, stuttering, "I am from Micholovce". "Oh, that is a nice place, and did you attend school there?" "Well, I did until the Nazis banned us from attending school", he answered.

He, calming down, and breathing in and out, asked her, "What have you been doing with yourself?" She answered with a princess-like demeanor and almost did an arabesque with her hands. With an assured tone in her voice, "I have had a private nanny who has tutored me".

"So you did!" the words sprung out spontaneously. He shook his head, but noticed that she was looking uncomfortable, so said, "I am sorry, I should not have asked you that question". She shrugged her shoulders. She cleared her voice, while she held her nose a little bit in the air, and said, "It doesn't matter to me what you think about rich people".

H thoughts scattered all over his mind. First, he wanted to tell her about his own home, which was a mansion; he remembered the large size of his own bedroom; He gripped his thoughts and remembered something that Martin had once told him, "We must show humility to God, no matter what, and especially now", and he felt a sense of assurance returning to his thoughts. He cleared his throat and said, "Well, I am not picking on rich people".

She smiled and asked the question, "Have you ever been rich?" He shrugged his shoulders and looked at her and he spoke in a very soft tone of voice, "I have forgotten to think about money". He looked down at the ground and then at the sky. He questioned her while looking at, "what is money, when you are hunted down like a dog?" She frowned, but Sam could see that she was not as affected by the war as he and his family had been.

She came closer to him. She looked at him for a minute with questioning eyes. She spoke in a soft tone of voice, "it has been hard for the last five years even for me and my family. He looked up at her and smiled, and she smiled back.

The both of them breathed in and out, and Sam cautioned her, my brother Martin always tells me when I feel like I am going to despair that, "We must remember in our hearts that we are Jews". She nodded her head as if to say, "yes", while tears came to her eyes. Sam stared at the sky. She stared at the same direction in the sky. They felt peace in their hearts.

The color of the sky was a light blue. There was not a cloud to be seen. No airplanes flying overhead as in most of Europe and now, recently in Slovakia. Miles of trees could be seen----the green colors and the shades of earth tones were spectacular. There were no trucks with the 'evil sign' and ruthless soldiers driving up to houses. No soldiers, marching like robots ready to shoot and kill, with no regard for human life could be seen. Sam commented, "this place is 'peaceful'; an oasis in time and space, in the middle of a world war, where the innocent are dying in startling numbers, which is considered a desert of oppression and depression, very much the opposite of an oasis. Oh, Let us bless G-d for granting us this 'momentous moment of peace'". She nodded with her head in affirmation, while she pressed her lips tightly together. Her blue eyes shined with rays of sympathy.

Many moments passed by. She broke the silence by asking, "What do you think you will do after the war?" Sam hesitated, and almost cried---his thoughts jumbled in his mind, he breathed in heavily for a minute and then he said, "It may never end". He cleared his throat, saying, "I just do not know".

"Well, I am going back to my house", she said with an attitude of confidence. He looked at her, questioningly, and in a soft tone of voice, said, "You never think that maybe your house will not be standing?" She quipped, "no, never" and made a grunting sound, "grrrr". He looked at her with amazement. She answered firmly in a loud voice: "the house will be standing".

Realizing that she was in denial, he said, "Well, all right then". "I was thinking", he said, as he snapped a branch off from a tree, and then paused. She coaxed him to answer her, in a questioning tone, "What were you thinking?" "I was thinking of becoming a jeweler," he said with a smile. "That sounds good to me", she said with her arms folded across her chest.

The color of the sky changed from an encouraging blue to a discouraging, dismal gray. The clouds were assembling and then massing. "Well, I must be going home", he said to her. She twisted her hips slightly and said, "You can stay for a while longer can't you?" "Well, I guess for a little while," and he paused and said, "looks like it is going to rain. I think I would like to get home before the down pour". "She waved her right hand in the front of her face and said, "Don't worry about it. You can always come to my hideout". He looked at her and smiled, and he asked, "are you sure that you have enough room?" "Of course we do", she answered most assuredly. The cloudiness faded just as suddenly as it had appeared. Like magic, the brightness of the sun shined brightly.

"How about we walk around the lake?" he asked her. Pausing, he said as he remembered what he wanted to ask her in the first place, "how about I ask you what your name is?" She looked at his eyes, her eyes glowing in the sunshine, and said softly, "Sarah". He smiled. Together they walked as they left their footprints in the sand----four feet with the same rhythm; that was the beat of their music. He looked at the ripples in the water, while she picked at some of the tops of the long grass. He spotted a school of fish swimming close to the surface of the water, and he knew that these were the fish of his survival. He smiled at her and she smiled back. There was a sense of warmth between them.

He was thinking, "wouldn't I like to hold her hand", and he thought some more, "her hand looks so delicate and gentle and it feels so cold". He concluded to himself, "she needs a strong man", and he sighed, "I am just the right one".

She was thinking, "with his pointed nose, and dark, wavy blond, light brown hair, and milk white skin, and blue eyes, he looks more handsome than a German", and she shook her head a few times up and down in affirmation. She looked at him and she frolicked in her thoughts, "he is so tall and handsome". "Hmm", I wonder what his name is", she said to herself.

They walked to the other side of the lake and then rested a few feet away from the edge. They looked at the lake, admiring its natural flow and watching the water flow, as they continued their walk. "What is your name?" she asked as she moved her head sideways. "Oh", he stammered, "my name is Samuel", and he pronounced his name with a voice of distinction. She smiled and nodded her approval.

Stopping where there was a clearing of the wild grasses, which spouted up and extended their tinsel apexes, red, grey, wheat, all different earth tone colors, towards the sky; Sam bent down and knelt to the edge of the water and cupped his left hand. Bringing the clear, pristine water to his mouth, he quickly supped up a handful of the water. He breathed in and out and wiped his mouth, saying, "this is really good, fresh-tasting water".

He saw her reflection in the water, flowing, flowing gently away with the ripples of the water of the lake. "Don't disappear on me", he said quietly to himself, and he got up and wiped his mouth.

Together, they gazed at the sky and stared quietly into the open and expansive space; both of them wishing for a peace and an end to the war. She spotted a shining, bright star and said, "I wish that I could reach up and pull down that star". Sam was amused at the thought, and laughed out loud.

She broke the silence by saying, "what are you going to eat for supper?" He hesitated, because his thoughts were not on food. He answered her, "most likely some of the mushrooms we had last night and maybe some berries and some pieces of flatbread". She exclaimed, "Never heard of that kind of bread". "Well, we have had to be resourceful and make what we can", he answered her with a choking sound in his voice. She paused and then asked, "Do you have anything to put on the bread?" "Oh, yes", we eat the bread with some of the quince preservatives my mother has made", he answered, thinking of all of the hard work that went into it. "Your mom must be a really good cook," she said. Sam smiled as a response, and he was so happy to hear Sara said that.

The blue skies gave way to a deepening gray color once again. Thunder roared like a lion had a tooth ache and lightening bolted like the sky was angry: all of these were a harbinger of an approaching storm that was going to have a downpour. The rain fell in its downpour a few minutes later. Sam's jacket got soaked in just a few minutes. Sarah's sweater was soaked wet too.

"Well, we had better get under some trees for cover", Sam declared. Sam spotted a cluster of old trees. "Come on with me over here", he called to Sarah. She followed and he covered her head and shoulders with his jacket, and they sat under the large trees together. They watched the rain falling. All of the leaves near them soon were covered with droplets of water. Occasionally, a rabbit would dart out of one of the nearby bushes. And the young couple would laugh at it.

They laughed a little; they talked a little; they sang a little; they cried together a little. Sam said, "I am hungry". Sarah said, "You must come to my hideout and eat with us. Sam hesitated, "well, all right, but only if you have enough food". Sarah quickly answered, "I know that we have enough food otherwise I would not have invited you".

"But how do you really know that?" Sam asked her with a concerned expression in his voice. "I know because once a month we get a delivery of canned food. We bury the cans and use them when we need them", she told him. If we are lucky, we get a delivery of fruits and fresh breads. The breads are so welcome. They remind of home. "Would you have any fresh bread?" Sam thought out loud and asked, but then caught his thoughts. Sarah answered with a smile on her face, "Yes. We do. It is rye bread. Do you like rye bread Sam?" she asked.

He answered without any doubt, as he was licking his lips, "Oh, yes. I love it". He paused for a moment, with his eyes protruding, and said, "I used to eat it all of the time with fresh butter". The rain shut off in the sky just as suddenly as the cloudy faucets had turned on.

The sun came out of hiding behind one of the puffy clouds. The rain stopped as suddenly as it began. There was the smell of fresh green leaves in the air. The fresh smell of the leaves and the thought of eating fresh, baked rye bread put expressions of joy on their faces.

They walked slowly side by side for a while. Sam stopped suddenly in his tracks. Sarah hesitated and then asked him, "Why are you stopping?" He replied curtly, "in case you do not know it—there is a war all around us".

She hesitated as though she was dazed, and then she looked into his eyes, and she said, "Oh, okay". "You must remember!" he cautioned her.

She walked first and then he followed, as she led him very carefully by the side of a ravine. Then up an ascending hill and when they reached a cluster of bushes, she said, "we are almost there". Sam cautioned her, as he held his finger on his closed lips, and she just stared at him, barely expressing any thoughts.

"You must not talk, and you must walk very softly," he cautioned, while whispering. She pointed to a direction to the north of them, saying, "Over there, see where there is the cluster of pine trees on the hill?" He looked for a few minutes, his right eye closed and his left eye protruding and focusing closer and closer as though he was adjusting a telescope, and he said slowly, "yes". She continued, "Well, there in the midst of the thick, strong-looking pine trees is our house; it is in the midst of the underbrush". "That sounds fantastic. Wow, what a place to hide". They walked for a bit.

"Okay, then lead me to your hideout", Sam said, as he broke the silence.

They walked up the steep hill and walked through the dozens and dozens of unseen, untouched pine trees, and almost tripped on the pine cones that had fallen beneath them; and there it was: thick brush and within the underbrush there was a large wooden house. It was almost like finding a sunken ship in the middle of the ocean. With hand hewn shutters, which had never been painted, which covered its windows so precisely; and noticeable thick planks of oak wood cut down, hewn, and chiseled for its door, the house stood still in time, most quietly, but assuredly, but majestically; a materialistic stature of wealth, which was an obvious indication of accomplishment attributable to hard work and sacrifice.

Looking ahead for only a short distance, he spotted a deserted figure of a man lying on the ground. Sam alerted Sarah, and they both walked over to the man. Sam exclaimed, "Why, it is a man, and he is breathing"; and at that moment, the man rolled over and opened his eyelids and stared at them, whimpering. Sam arched his neck in a downward direction and asked, "Would you like to come with us for food?" The man answered in a weak tone of voice, "Yes. I am very hungry," and he sat up. "Just follow us", Sam exclaimed. The man walked slower than Sam, but hobbled along, favoring his right leg.

As they reached the clearing near the house, Sarah's sister, Molly, ran out, waving her left hand and calling out loudly, "hello". She spotted the 'stranger'. She stopped where she stood, staring with her eyes instinctively and putting her hands on her breasts. Her mouth was opened and she looked like she was going to scream. Sam blurted out, "Do not be afraid. He will not harm you. He has come for some food. Molly's sister stopped still, while gripping her hands. Sam said to the stranger, "come with us and we will get you some food". Molly's sister exclaimed in an indignation tone of voice, "No, no." I do not want him in my house." Sam held back what he wanted to say while gritting his teeth. There was a 'dark silence for more than a moment. He could not talk to Molly. He said to the stranger, "Stay here. I will bring you some food".

Sarah's dad put down the lace curtain. He said to Sam and Sarah, "welcome, welcome. You are just in time for some venison and potatoes", and he patted Sam on the back. Sam rubbed his hands and said, "I will be back in a minute. He walked to the stranger and gave him the fish that he had caught, and he gave him a plate of venison and potatoes, saying to the stranger, "here take this, and God be with you". The stranger looked at him with reverberating circles in his eyes, but grateful they were grateful expressions in his eyes; he grabbed the fish and grabbed the plate of cooked venison and potatoes, and he ran down the hill, and ran into the woods into his own hiding place.

Sam looked all around the outside of the house carefully. When he was sure that no one had followed, he put up his right thumb. Sarah moved quickly to the front door and twisted the handle quickly. Together they made a quick entrance and closed the door just as quickly behind them. Both of them sighed from relief, as they walked into the large living room, which had five medium-sized wooden chairs for couches. Small-hand-sewn quilts were hung on the top of the chairs and other quilts were placed for seat cushions, providing décor somewhat in the manner that they were used to living in.

"I will call my mother and my father", Sarah announced. Sam nodded. In a few moments, there was the sound of two simultaneously sounding voices announcing, "So you are Sarah's friend. And in the same sentence they announced, "Come, join us for some supper".

Sam was dazzled when he saw that the dining room table almost took up the entire space of the room. Large size wooden chairs surrounded the table. The smell of fresh baked bread came from the room on the side, which was the kitchen. They sat down at the table, while Sarah's father said the blessing and cut the bread. Sarah's mother offered strawberry jelly for the bread.

"Where do you come from?" The father asked, as he sat way back in his high-arched chair. Sam answered, "My family had to escape from the Germans. We have been hiding in the woods nearby."

"The Nazis, the Germans, Hitler, they are all the same! Rotten to do what they are doing to the Jews!" he exclaimed, and his face turned red in color and he almost choked on the piece of bread that he had in his mouth. His wife bowed down her head, praying in silence.

Sam shook his head in bewilderment. Sara did not utter a word, as she stared through the lace curtain, watching as the man seemed to have the strength to run through the trees. They sat at the kitchen table and talked about the news. "So where do you think Hitler is today?" Sarah's father, Jonah asked. Sam answered, "Hopefully deep in Russia with his armies dying off quickly from starvation and the bitter cold. As long as he is away from Czechoslovakia, we have hope that the war will end soon!" They all raised their cups and said a toast, "May we all survive." Sam cleared his throat and ate quickly. "Not so fast eating your food---you must savor every morsel of the food", Jonah called out, as they all shoveled the food into their mouths. Sam smiled and nodded his head.

He looked at Sam and asked, "Would you like a cup of homemade tea?" Sam drank a cup of homemade tea and sat and talked with Jonah for another fifteen minutes about his father's lumber business. Sara and her mother cleared the table. Molly swept the floor.

The man looked at Sam, whose eyes were beginning to close and he said, "Young man, let me get you something from the kitchen for you to take home with you". "Well, it is getting late and I must be going on my way," Sam said, as he pushed the chair away from the table slowly.

The man had several handfuls of sugar cookies wrapped in a checkered cloth, large blue and white colored cloth. "Here", he said. "This will bide your time on your way home and there are plenty of extras". "Yes, yes. Thanks so much", Sam answered and he immediately took one of the cookies to chew on. Sam eyed another cookie and then closed the cloth checkered cloth and put the cookies into his coat pocket.

As he left the house, Sam felt a somewhat silence feeling and he shivered. Sam shrugged his shoulders as if he did not understand the silence, but continued a fast pace, because he knew it was not safe to be alone in the woods at night or day. He wondered about the war and wondered if the Nazis would ever discover the house, which was in the middle of the pine trees. "Better to have an underground bunker", he muttered to himself. He questioned, "Was it real or was it an enchanted house?" He threw his hands up in the air and walked on. His feet did their job almost automatically. His mind began to think of Jewish history. The indomitable fortress of Masada entered his mind. The Romans succeeded in conquering the fortress after a long siege. "But the people held on to the last minute," he said to himself. What about Queen Esther? She conquered a Haman single-handed. Sam's thoughts came back to reality; Sam felt his forehead, because it was beginning to throb. "Must not get too upset," he cautioned himself.

It took him less time to come home than it took to find the house. This was the first time in a long while that his feet ached. He announced to his family, "There is another family living just three miles up the trail." He showed the cookies to his family. Everyone took one and expressed how good the cookies tasted. No one asked questions why he had been gone so long. They sat for a while quietly all together. Occasionally one person looked at another, but for the most part there was silence for at least an hour. Anna initiated a thought, "I wish that I could visit some of my family". No answer from anyone.

They all sat for a while. Joseph got up and asked, "Who will go with me to find our breakfast?" Silence, and Joseph did not pursue it. Martin, after a few minutes, initiated, "I will go with you". Joseph nodded his head. Soon they were on their way. Fishing poles in their hands.

Anna asked, "Would you like some of the supper?" Sam answered quickly, "Yes, I am hungry", and he sat quietly on the crudely hewn kitchen stool and rested his elbows softly on the crudely hewn kitchen table. Mushrooms, which were dipped in wild berry sauce was the supper. Sam gobbled it all down. Sam was up early the next morning. He said to Anna, "I am going to pick berries". She nodded and looked at him with a strong sense of awe and admiration.

Sam emerged from their well-built tunnel for escape and entered the whirlpool of the German net that was ever present in his mind, and, of course, was real. He knew. He knew that he had to remember her name. He headed for the lake. He headed to see her, Sara. He said to himself over and over again, Sara, Sara, Sara, and he started to hum and he felt happy.

Near the lake, he picked some berries and put them in his knapsack. When he got to the lake, he fashioned a string by twisting three strong vines and cutting them with his pen knife; he attached the vine to a pole that he had made by cutting off a long and tall branch from a beech tree and he left the pole where he could easily find it on the side of the lake. When he came to the lake and sat at the edge of the lake he fished.

She was swimming in the water and she saw him and waved. She came out and wiped her body, starting from her hair and then her breasts and working her way down to her toes. She bent down to wipe off her toes. She quickly wrapped the towel around herself. He continued to fish and made believe that he had not noticed her. She dressed quickly into the same outfit. She walked over to him and sat down beside him and they both watched the water for a sign of a bubble or a bob of the fishing pole. "Sometimes it is hard to catch a salmon or a grayling", she said.

"Once in a while a big salmon lurks by, but it is hard to catch one, because they are a very large size fish, maybe even two feet long". Just as Sara was describing the salmon fish, which is unique to the river waters and streams in Czechoslovakia, the pole jutted upwards and moved sideways about 190 degrees. Sam's hand suddenly was jerked as the fishing pole was being pulled down into the water, but slowly----being pulled into the ripples of the lake. Suddenly, in space of two minutes, white clear, iridescent bubbles emerged to the top of the water----and, behold, like magic, a fish could be seen just about coming up to the surface. "Oh, a fish", she exclaimed, with a rush of pink color to her face. "Yep, and not too hard to catch either", and he pulled the fish out of the water. It was not hard. He gave the pole one hard pull and up into the air the fish flew. But the fish was strong and fought back. The fish pulled mightily and tugged mightily until Sam thought that he might have to let him go! He backed away from the lake and the more the fish was away from the water, the less chance of surviving it had. Sam smiled and said, "Well, I guess that we will have fish for dinner after all". They parted for the day. She went to her hideout and he went to his.

Sam and Sara had agreed to meet once a week; and it worked out nicely for both of them. Then there would be the Sabbath to look forward to. So the boredom and the fears did not eat away at his conscious self. Another six months of the war had gone by.

In the morning of this next day, Sam said to his mother, "I must go fishing today", and he trekked through the woods, fully clothed with a warm jacket and pants. Anna did not question herself, "why" she only wondered when Sam would bring Sara over to his own family's bunker and introduce her to his family. She could not help feeling that she had a feeling, a strange feeling in, a shaking feeling within her that something was going to happen; most of the time she dismissed these feelings. But this time, she called Martin and said, "See if you can follow your brother" and as she hesitated, she said, "in case he needs you". Martin followed Sam through all of the trails through all of the pine woods and beech woods and did not lose him even though he stayed far behind Sam.

Sam headed straight to the lake. The wind blew on his back and he said, "Wind, wind blow at me some more and faster, and he ran faster, while looking for Sara from a distance. Sarah was sitting on a log, waiting for him at the lake, at the usual spot, beyond the clearing. Puffing and huffing, his cheeks almost red like a red-colored apple, he walked up to her and said, "How are you?" She turned her head and said, "I am okay" in a soft, sad-sounding voice. They sat for a while. She gave him three left over sugar cookies; and while biting on one, he put the others in his jacket pocket and patted the outside of the pocket in an automatic response.

He fished and she sat next to him and together they watched the string at the end of the pole. She saw the water move in circles with the circles floating farther away from the center circle. As she watched, she began to see glimpses of her life---living in her home---running up and down the twenty-five steps on the stairway, inviting her friends over to do their homework together, going together as a family every Saturday to the temple, coming home from the temple and having a discussion on the part of the Bible that the Rabbi discussed. Her thoughts were interrupted as Sam suddenly called out, "wow, this is a big fish. He tugged at the line and tried to pull it in. Sarah watched, her eyes bulging, as she jumped up and down in excitement. She said, "This time, you have really caught a big one. You have caught a salmon". "Yes". He answered back. "My idea of tying four big worms to an old shell surely worked. He got up and danced. He held her and they danced. They were happy.

At a hill a short distance away, which was well hidden from the pathway that had been formed by the people, hunters, and people who were hiding, who trekked through this terrain, Martin watched. He smiled and looked in amazement and thought, "my brother Sam has found a girlfriend, and I think that it is going to grow into a serious relationship----and of all places---in the middle of the woods. Contented that he had solved the riddle of who this captivating maiden was, Martin headed home to the hideout, on guard always for Nazis or collaborators.

His mother greeted him with swelled excitement, saying, "So what happened, so what happened?" Martin blurted out with one quick breath, "Sam has found a girlfriend and I think that it is serious". "No, but I will tell you that I knew that he found a friend but I did not know that it would be serious. You know Sam, he is always clowning around, no?" Anna questioned. "Yes," Martin answered, and Anna stepped backwards and sat down on one of the wooden living room chairs and took out a cloth handkerchief and blew her nose, and for a while she sat and stared into space, but she was smiling. Martin broke the silence by saying, "It will be all right." She looked up at him, and she nodded, "yes", but there were tears in her eyes.

Not far from the lake, and close to some large boulders from the magnificent Carpathian Mountains; and only a short distance from their hideout in the woods, Sara's sister had begun taking sunbaths, just to pass the time of day. She had fashioned foil paper around a large piece of cardboard, and while she sat in a wooden chair, she held the cardboard under her chin. She closed her eyes, and she supped in the warmth of the sun. Sarah's sister had somehow forgotten that a horrible war was raging.

The sun's reflection bounced from the cardboard to the nearby boulders of the mountain many times during the day, then up into the ridges of the mountains many times just like the sound of an echo. As the sun got hotter, the reflection bounced off from one rock to the other more and more. She was completely unaware of the danger she was putting herself in. Per chance, the sun's rays announced the family's presence, signaling telegraphically, "We are here."

Unknown to most of the local people and known only to the loyal collaborators with the local Nazi organization and with the Czech Priest who befriended Hitler, Father Tiso, the Nazis were looking over the terrain; they were looking for partisans who might be hiding; they were looking for Russian soldiers who might be regrouping; and they were looking for American soldiers who might be thinking of liberating Czechoslovakia and the Germans were always fearful of losing their power in Czechoslovakia; it meant a loss of some of the richest natural resources in the world: the forest alone produced invaluable pine wood and beech wood; the country was wealthier than most other European countries-----its ownership of solid gold bullion was a staggering amount! And strategically, Czechoslovakia was not a good country to lose because it was land-locked and bordered six other countries, including Poland. The country of Poland was of super military strategic value to the Germans because logistically it was a route to conquering Russia, a goal that they demanded within themselves to achieve.

On that same afternoon, a handful group of Nazi soldiers, five soldiers, were on patrol, surveying the top of the mountain and every once and a while they used their binoculars to look at different directions of the Carpathian Mountains. While they descended the mountain, one of the soldiers spotted the reflection of the sun shining off and on onto one of the boulders like it was a signal.

"What is that?" He yelled out loudly as he pointed to the reflection. His lieutenant quickly peered through his binoculars. He said in a bitter-sounding voice, "Cannot see exactly where it is coming from, but we must find out from where!" He yelled to his men, "Could be a signal from a Russian or a partisan, or a Yid!" He quickly ordered everyone to search. He led the way, with his hand nesting on an open holster, and his mindset was ready to shoot, no matter what.

The clouds had grown gray and Molly, noticing that the weather had changed, she thought, "Must be going home." She folded the sun board, and brushed off her clothes. As she walked, she stopped to pick wild purple flowers, and she thought; "I will bring these home for my mother." She was unsure what to do with the sun board. She hid it in one of the nearby bushes, but left the wooden chair. She started to walk home. She was half way there when, the Germans discovered the chair. They searched the bushes and then they found the sun board. They thought of the sun board as a signal board and were immediately on the alert for a fugitive. They saw her footprints and they followed them. They followed her and reached her before she had reached her house.

A shot from one of their shotguns whizzed out. It pierced her head. Stunned, she stood still, shaking--her body grew instantly colder. The soldiers ran down the pathway so quickly, reaching her, crushing tiny white flowers with the weight of their big, ferocious boots. Five tall, green-clad soldiers surrounded her, each soldier aiming his rifle at her head.

"Where are you from?" the German lieutenant shouted. She stood and stared at the soldiers, not believing what she saw. Cold and shaking, her lips changed to a shade of purple from blue. "Where are you from?" the lieutenant shouted again and before she could muster up the strength to answer, the lieutenant walked up to her and slapped her in the face. His impatience grew and he slapped her two more times.

She fell to the ground. Her hand accidentally brushed against his rifle. Acting only on animal instinct, one of the soldiers fired his gun at her. She lay on the ground where she fell, lifeless.

"Why did you do that?" the lieutenant shouted at the soldier. The soldier stood at attention and answered, "These Jews are not that smart". The lieutenant stared at the soldier and then laughed. He shouted, "We will find her hideout. Make it quick", as his eyes automatically surveyed the surrounding area and he left with one of the soldiers for high ground.

The three German soldiers followed the pathway, walking on the fallen grasses and leaves. The wooden house, squelched between tall, thick pine trees, slowly was discovered through the spaces in-between the briars which deftly covered it. Smoke was obvious from its chimney. The sharp eyes of one of the German soldiers spotted it. The soldiers banged down the wooden door on the front of the house. Their rifle butts loosened the door instantly and bore large and misshaped gores and chips into the skilled craftsmanship of the door; unable to resist their unnatural force, the door crashed to the floor, and once the door was opened, the opened space revealed both Sara's mother and father. The two shivering figures hovered together as fear was written on their protruding eyes. Their heart beats could be heat a distance away.

The soldier in charge shouted, "let us finish this disgusting job today. Shoot them!" Two lifeless figures fell. They lay cold on the creaking wooden planks of the living room floor; they remained an imprint in time, testifying to the German soldiers' vulgarity and cruelty. I am certain that their last words expounded that they were innocent of any wrong doings and that they questioned, "Why are you doing this to me?"

From the distance, Sarah and Sam heard the rifle shots; at first dazed by the meaning of the shots, and unable to discern its full impact and meaning. Sam grasped the reality, though, a few minutes later, and he bit his lips. He grabbed Sara by the hand and held her tightly. "Do not go," he yelled, while his head moved in every direction, trying to sense if the Germans were coming near them. She struggled with him, pulling her hand away, until she broke from his grip. She cried out, "I must go to my family," while tears clouded her eyes.

"You must be quiet and you must hide", he quickly responded in an almost harsh tone of voice, and he grabbed her by the arm. She tugged with him for several minutes and pushed him away. She ran to her family. He called to her, "come back" with frightening thoughts palpating in his heart. She ran swiftly and was soon out of sight.

Sam stopped in his tracks, knowing the dangers. After a few minutes, he bowed down his head. Thoughts rushing through his mind, he knew, nevertheless, to follow his instincts. He ran to hide under some thick brush. Through the thickness of entangled vines, he heard the sound of three shots—identifying death, loss of life, loss of his beloved; he realized that the Germans had killed her. He realized that they were all gone. He cried like a baby---stopping only when his breathing had became belabored. He knew that he had to escape. He did not want to be their fifth victim. He knew that they had the guns and that he was outnumbered. He cried to himself, "Why didn't she listen to me?"

Nighttime fell with a deep cold chill, and he knew that the darkness would give him a better chance for escape. His mind turned to prayers---reciting what he could remember of the evening prayers. He dried his tears and was about to stand up when he heard the sound of leaves cracking, and the "woof, woof" sound of a dog.

Shaking with fright, he crawled deeper into another patch of thicker brush, and there were some wild berries, scratching his body innumerable times with wounds bleeding, but he knew that he had to hide; he lay quietly for at least an hour; his posture in a fetal position. Torn by the thorns of the brush, he suddenly remembered that if he crushed some berries, his scent would be gone; he quickly rubbed the berries into the fabric of his clothes. He rubbed the crushed berries on his hair. He rubbed the berries all over his feet and all over his hands.

The ominous sound of the crackling leaves got louder. A dog barked.

"Is it one dog or two dogs?" Sam asked himself. He shuddered and prayed, saying the words, "help me God," over and over. The sound of the dog's bark came closer to the brush. Determining that it was only one dog, he sighed with relief. The dog sniffed in the air and stopped for a second and then he charged with front legs leaping forward----catching the scent of a white, brown-spotted rabbit.

The soldiers, running quickly after the dog, jutted up and down, the flaps of fat on their midriffs bouncing with a rhythm, up and down and then again. In no time the tune of their boots changed pace to almost a stop, as they were tugged down by the pull of the muddy surface—the hands of the 'dead' reaching and stretching to pull them into the ground with the help of the wind.

Sam never looked back. He had only a little more to go when the back of his legs throbbed with aching pain. He felt alone in a conquered wilderness, silhouetted by the disappearing moon, a disappearing glow in the dark, his only light. Bending his head while rubbing the back of his legs, thoughts rushing to his mind like, "could he have saved her", he threw himself down to his knees. He cried out for his friend, Sara. He cried out, "I have grown to love her". His heart was racing. He lay prostrate, attached to the ground, as though he belonged to the ground too. An owl perched high up in one of the surrounding trees, began to hoot. The composition of the music of the night opera of the deep woods continued throughout the night.

Martin thought he had heard the quick, piercing sound of the bullets finding its unfortunate marks---like small shooting arrows on fire, flying high in the distant wind, whizzing by at such an incredible speed. The bullets were like the fierce, well-aimed arrows from the warring tribes when the story of the Bible was being written. Following the sound of the hooting owl, and peering through open spaces between branches between the pine trees, he sighed out of relief when he finally spotted Sam. He walked slowly through the few unshorn, tall grasses, and knelt down beside his brother, while listening to the sounds of the music from the opera of the night.

Sam was lying prostrate, his form crushing the tall grasses beneath him. Martin reached for Sam's arm and helped him get up. Sam began to cry. "Save your tears brother, until we are safe", Martin cautioned him. Sam, out of anger, pushed Martin away. They struggled for a few minutes, and Sam fell, saying, "I have nothing to live for", and he covered his face with his hands. The night grew even darker as Martin tugged at Sam's arm and helped him get up. Martin prompted him, "Come on. Come on brother. Let us get out of here!"

Sam grunted and walked at a slow pace. "Let me be", Sam called out. Martin answered firmly, "No. Never give in to the Nazis". "They are everywhere", Sam said as he leaned his head backwards. Martin, squeezed his eyes shut, stepped backwards a few paces and he held his lips tightly together. He said firmly in a soft tone of voice, "Our Lord will deal with the Nazis. You will see! You must have faith."

"Oh, will he? He laughed loudly, as though he was inebriated. Saliva collected in his mouth and he bent forward and spit out. He watched the saliva seep into the ground. He saw a flash of light coming toward the two of them suddenly. Martin was unsure whether to hide or not. He was unsure whether the light was real or unreal. Faces started to come forward. Whole bodies walked out of the muddy earth. The bare bodies gathered and huddled together, men and women and children; they danced, holding outstretched hands and they turned round and round and round. Stopping for a minute, they swayed from side to side and then clapped their hands and tapped their feet to the melody of the music that was in the night. Slowly the light faded. He gathered his courage. He said to Sam, "Come on brother, let us get out of this place".

Smoke appeared, coming from small pipes that were installed into the conduit on ground on the other side of the cave. Slowly, the smoke inched up to the tops of their heads and then covered them. In a moment, the music of the night that was in their minds, stopped, and they were all falling to the ground. Sam's vision blurred because he had so many tears. But he wiped away the tears and carried his brother on his shoulder; they were on their way home.

Sam closed his eyes, afraid to open them. Martin shook him, as Sam's head and shoulders went back and forth, and then back and forth again, and he cried, "Come on, come on. Wake up brother." Sam opened his eyes, and he blurted, " I just do not know why they were all killed by the Nazis". While lifting up his arms, he called out, "help me God. Help me brother". Tears fell from Martin's eyes, as he gulped, barely able to mutter the words, "yes". He bent down and reached for Sam's hands. Sam was able to walk by himself now.

Sam staggered as Martin walked by his side. The distance to their bunker home was not far, but it seemed like every moment was an hour. Martin broke the silence, as he spotted the opening of the underground bunker. "It is tragic, but you must go on." And he said firmly, "But you must go on, because you are a Jew". Choked up with tears, Sam muttered, "Yes, I am a Jew", and then, shuddering, he held his head down and wept bitterly. Sam cried out, "She was a Jew, too!" Sam's leg's weakened, and his knees throbbed, and he beckoned Martin, "Can we sit a little bit?" Martin shook his head for a moment, clearly expressing "No". "You know the story. The longer we sit and talk, the longer we set ourselves up as targets". Sam nodded his head up and down in approval and said, with a murmur in the tone of his voice, "She was so young. She was so beautiful". He sobbed, "I loved her. Brother, I loved her."

Martin answered him, as he crouched down and sat on the sandy ground, "you must remember that you are a Jew and that there is a purpose for you on this earth. You will remember her."

"Oh, what purpose is there for me?" Sam asked with an agitated tone in his voice. "Yes, God is always with us even though it seems like he has abandoned us", Martin told him. Sam got up to his feet and questioned, "Tell me, what Sara did that was so very wrong?" Martin spoke in a firm tone of voice, "God is good and God is merciful…. The Germans killed Sara and her family and the Germans are certainly not Jews". Sam smiled a small smirk, as he said, "no, I guess not, and then he said, in a more serious tone of voice, "They are Germans, devils in disguise, but the horns and the thorns are there". "Yes, they are, and our God has quite a job on his hands saving his people from the throes of the devil," Martin answered. Sam breathed in and out and felt better. The brothers walked on, side-by-side.

After at least a half hour had gone by, Martin paused and said, in a calm tone of voice said, "God's messengers, the angels just cannot be everywhere in the same time". Sam was much calmer now, but tired and said, "Okay, but I think I need to rest". Martin replied quickly, "Come with me, my brother and let us live; let us escape to our hideout, and let us live to see the day when the devil is completely subdued by God and his angels. Sam muttered, "I say Amen to that", and Martin put his hand on the top of Sam's shoulder, and they walked together towards the hideout. Sam was almost like an inanimate stick, propelled by a physical force of motion at first. Then thoughts raced to Sam's mind about Sara. He called out, "Martin, she could have become my wife. She could have borne my children. We could have walked together to the synagogue; she could have sat on the other side of the curtain."

"Yes, that is true", Martin said, as he wondered if Sam was able to go any further. "We will rest for a minute, and we will talk, but only for a minute," he cautioned Sam. Martin thought and then spoke, "I cannot answer your question, even though I agree with your thoughts". He paused and then he said, "Think back to the beginning of our history-- that has been handed down from generation to generation---Jacob entered the 'promised land' after much strife." "What does that all mean?" Sam questioned, as he looked up to Martin. "It means that there are bad people and that there are good people and this is the way that it has been for centuries", Martin said. "Do you think that the curse will end?" Sam questioned. Martin looked up to the stars and paused for a moment, and he sighed, "I think that God wants the hatred to stop, but has not figured out how to make people want to love. Of one thing I am certain---God chose us as his chosen people. We are a people whom are loved by God." He paused and then smiled as he said with a comforting sound in his voice, "I know that one day there will be peace in which everyone will want to participate", and Martin cried softly to himself. Martin blew his nose and wiped the tears from his eyes with his cotton handkerchief and announced, "Hopefully the forces of good will subdue the forces of evil soon", and he paused and then said, "I would like to sing, maybe even be a cantor, and maybe even write a book". Sam asked, "But what would you write a book on?" "Oh, that is simple," he paused and nodded his head in affirmation of his thoughts, "why I would write a book about us brothers and our mother and father and sister". Sam asked, "Would it be about the war?" Martin answered, "Oh, yes".

Sam chuckled as he said, "I would like to be a jeweler". I would like to see the glitter and glow of gems." "Well, there you have the idea—we will live through this horrible war if we keep our wits together. We will survive. Let us go now brother, please," Martin said to Sam.

They had the hideout in sight, when Sam faltered and missed his step and almost fell to the ground. Martin coaxed him, "come on brother, like mom always says, 'the camps, the camps'. Sam we got to live, we have to fight for survival, because otherwise we will end up in the concentration camp, the camps."

"Will we ever live a life without fear?" Sam asked, as he closed his eyes for a minute, but kept his feet moving---first the right foot and then he put the left foot forward. Martin answered, "You and I, we have to hope, otherwise the game of life is over".

Sam said, "Martin, sing something to me." "You got to be kidding—in the middle of the woods with Germans creeping and crawling around, no thanks," Martin puffed the words out of his mouth.

Sam stopped cold and cried, "Brother, I need you to sing the song about the Messiah coming". Martin paused and pursed his lips and said, "I will sing it softly", and he chanted the words, "the Messiah is coming. We will all be free". He sang the words over and over again.

Thoughts rushed through Sam's mind, however, and he cried, while shaking his hands in the air, "I have to go back to bury them. I just have to". "Hold on, brother, we are here to be together, to survive together", Martin said with kindness and understanding with a soft expression and concern in his voice. "I must go back, I must go back", Sam protested.

"You will go back when we tell you it is safe to go back, and you will not go alone!" Martin said in an adamant tone of voice, and he asked, "Do you understand that?" Sam continued to cry. He would not move.

Martin said, "Stay here and don't move". Martin ran to the hideout and tapped the signal, five taps on the opening. Joseph heard the signal, and he tapped one time back. Martin went back to Sam and waited with him. He knew that his father would find them soon. Sam gave in to his weary body and fell asleep. Martin sat down beside him and waited.

After a short while, Martin heard a strange rustling noise through the grasses; he looked up and spotted his father walking around them. He knew to wait quietly. Shortly, Joseph appeared in front of them suddenly, at first like a shadow in the back of a dark curtain. His finger was pointing to his mouth, and Martin shook his head, and nodded "Yes" that he understood.

Joseph and Martin grabbed Sam by the arm and walked with him; they pulled him down into the hideout. Martin puffed out a large sigh of relief, when he bolted down the hideout door.

Sam slumped to the floor, despondent, his face colored ruddy red. He lay for two days, hardly moving his body; it was his own form of hibernation from life. On the third day, he opened his eyes; he looked around the room as though in a daze, and cried out, "I am hungry." Everyone stood by his side and smiled at him.

Anna brought him a wooden bowl filled with broth, which she had made from the roots of nearby plants and had cooked a wild bird in it. She made sure that Sam sipped it all as she sat with him.

Joseph told her, "Bernard and Martin, and I will find the bodies and bury them when it is safe". He paused, and shook his head, trying to overcome the sadness.

Sam muttered in his sleep, "I loved her, I loved her". The rain came in torrents the next night, and Joseph said to Bernard and Sam, "the

Nazis will not be roaming through the woods in the height of the storm. Besides," he pointed out, "Martin will be the watchman while Bernard and I dig the graves". "Won't the ground be rather hard in late October?" Anna queried, while she sat arched in her chair. Her eyes glazed with fright as her eyes opened wider. Joseph answered her, "I think the rain will protect us and will soften the ground". And he paused and then said, "Anyway, we don't expect to be there very long!"

They exited the hideout one by one, each waiting a few minutes until they were sure they were not being watched. They walked separately, with a good distance between themselves. They had rehearsed the way so that they knew exactly where they were going, in case one of them got lost. They had a signal, the sound of a bird cawing, if they spotted any trouble, and they knew to lie down and hide.

It was not until two hours later that the three men came upon the fallen bodies. The bodies appeared lifelike, lying in the rain with their swollen eyes wide open. The blood from their wounds had washed away in the rain. Joseph and his sons knew their task was gruesome, but it had to be done. Joseph used a large branch like a shovel and he started digging one large grave for the family. Martin positioned himself on the top of a nearby ledge and crouched down. Bernard stood next to his father and watched as the earth was slowly moved and the grave opened into a wide, deep pit. Joseph was nearly done when he felt something metal-like under his shovel. He said to Bernard, "You dig now and find out what is buried here!" Bernard dug around the metal object and then went into the large crevice and wiped the dust off of a large metal box. Bernard lifted the metal box by himself and placed it on the ground on the top of the crevice.

The box had rusted slightly on each of the side corners, but it stood solid. Bernard spoke with a sense of anticipation, "I wonder what is in this box?" Joseph replied with excitement rushing through his veins, "Well, open up the box and let us find out!" A gush of air rushed at them as the lid was quickly removed. They peered in and both expressed a sense of 'awe' at the same time, "why, it is cans of food and jars of cookies, and there is some money!" Bernard smiled and looked at Joseph and asked, "What should we do?" "I will tell you in one sentence" Joseph responded with a tone of decision and said, "Leave the box where it is, while we will bury the family".

When the ground was covered with a top layer of crumbled earth, and they had finished the prayers that they were able to remember, Joseph made the sound that was the signal. Martin knew to come over quickly. "Look, it is a shame to leave this food. The food will only rot or the Germans will find it and have a feast on it" Joseph said, and he continued, "Stuff your pockets, stuff your bandanas. Hide the tin box, and let us get out of this place!"

They ran at first from the scene of death, never looking back. When they had reached some distance in the woods, they slowed down their pace and walked single file. The trail had guided them along their way through circuitous, but parallel perimeters, inundated with overgrown brush. All three carried somber expressions on their faces. Their eyes, dazed with fright, were aimed straight and sometimes looked up to the sky for guidance.

They were more aware than ever that they were alive. Silently, they renewed their prayers to survive and to be free. Almost home, Joseph muttered to himself, "tragic waste of life". He collected his thoughts and squatted with an arched back, as he said to his sons, "I want you to tell Sam that we buried the family in the best way we could".

Bernard asked, "Should we tell about the food that we found?" "Tell no one nothing. Tell no one!" Joseph said in an adamant voice. His sons bowed their heads simultaneously and replied, softly, "yes". They reached the entrance of the hideout, but lingered for a while in the nearby woods. When they were certain that they had not been followed, they descended into the safety of the bowels of their underground bunker.

Anna swept her feet across the hardened ground, crying, as she said in a garbled, anxious voice, and she held out her hands, "come and have some hot coffee to the three men." All three men nodded their heads in an upward motion, and they sat down with somber expressions on their faces at the wooden kitchen table.

A new day with hope began after a restless night. Just before the rising of the dawn, blasts of cannon roared their fierce, explosive force in the distance beyond the woods abutting the Carpathian Mountains. Joseph, and Martin, and Bernard awoke with a shudder. Sam rolled over in his bed, snoring, adding to the noise of the cannons.

Anna started to cry. Edith sat on the ground next to her mother—not even an inch separated her body from Anna's, as Anna held her tightly. Joseph sat in his chair, staring at the opening of the cave. They all stayed where they were for at least two hours.

Through a crevice in the wall, a rat nervously ran out of its hiding place and ran nervously towards them. Edith screamed. Joseph and Martin ran around the room after it, cornering it as it neared the opening. Martin stepped on the rat with a fierce stomp, and the rat was silenced.

Joseph climbed up the short distance to the opening. He opened up the hatch and threw the dead rat in the distance. Pink lines in the sky caught his eyes and gray-colored blasting smoke filled his nostrils. The sound of the blasts was deafening and frightening, making his body shake. The sound of bombs bursting, and rifles shooting, and the disheartening, echoing sounds of the wounded made Joseph say to himself, "no good, the war must be closer than I thought," and he closed the hatch door and came down the ladder.

CHAPTER 14

TWO DESERTERS JOIN THEM

Sam muttered to himself, "Even the rats can't stand the noise." He put on his coat and hat and announced that he was going out to get some food. He didn't care if anyone heard him or not. He had gone out to get us some food, but he had to smell freedom in the air. But instead, he smelled the stench of war: the cannon smoke, the breath from dying soldiers, the burning of tanks and petrol, the burning of human flesh, and the shooting of dying animals. He knew that he could not go further into the woods for the Germans might be lurking there, but he shook his head out of disappointment.

He searched the area carefully for soldiers, and when he did not see any soldiers, he went about a mile deeper into the woods----into the underbrush, but still near a small stream; the stream he repeated to himself was his lifeline and compass; he was looking for a small rabbit or a squirrel, but he soon began to realize that he was not going to catch one this day.

He said, "Wild onions or mushrooms will have to do". He had bent down and picked quite a few wild onions and wild mushrooms and was ready to go home to the bunker when suddenly, he heard the snap of a twig. He turned his body in a pivotal movement, a click, an instant 180 degrees and listened carefully for any other sounds. Behold: there will be rabbit stew tonight. The rabbit, a brown one, had a thick coat of long fur, and very active, hopping legs----which had long white spots of white, jumped right out in front of him. Sam aimed his small knife carefully and most steadily, holding his feet firmly on the ground, and the small knife hit its mark. Joyful, he packed up the rabbit with the mushrooms and onions and headed home.

Not too far away, about fifty yards away, two men had heard the rustling noises. They were dressed in Nazi uniforms. One was very tall, well over six feet and the other one was short, around five feet four inches. They had deserted together from the Nazi army. They walked quickly and most carefully and even though Sam walked very carefully, they saw him in the far distance. They watched him like two swooping hawks. They followed him. When he was no longer in sight, they assumed that he was in his hiding place. They searched the brush. They looked for smoke. They looked for water holes. They looked for openings under the roots of trees. They could not find him. They decided to stay in the area, though, because they knew that he just could not have disappeared. They made a fire, warmed themselves, ate some provisions that they had managed to wrestle away from the Nazi army and they went to sleep right there and then, easily.

The next morning, they awoke as soon as the sun rose and they talked it over and they decided to leave the area completely. They felt that the German army might come back and they did not wish to be found. However, being hungry, the tall one sniffed the air and smelled a trace of smoke, and he said, "that young man is cooking that rabbit", and they both knew that when they found out where the smoke was coming from that they would find Sam's hideout; the two deserters looked over the brush again, sniffing constantly like hound dogs for the scent.

It took them quite a while to find the smoke. It was only when they started to follow the thick, interwoven brush downhill that they discovered a mist coming out of the ground. When they sniffed the air, they realized that this was the air vent attached to a stove. They searched the underbrush for an opening and after going through one branch after another and then another and then another, just like a designed time machine, they found the opening to the back door of the bunker and they opened it.

Joseph immediately knew that someone had entered the back way for the bells that were set up began to chime and this alerted the family immediately. Anna remained with Joseph, but the five children waited quietly in another underground room. The two soldiers boasted as they quickly approached Joseph and Anna, "We are hungry. We will take the food you are cooking". Joseph said quietly to them, "You are most welcome to share a piece with us".

The two deserters looked at each other and then the taller one said, "We think you have to give the food to us". Joseph cleared his throat and said, "We have been watching you for some time". He cleared his throat and wiped his lip with his clean cloth towel and said, "You must be deserters". The two men looked at each other and the taller one said, "So what?"

"Well, that means that you are not Nazis, but that you are fugitives from the Nazis". Joseph motioned for them to come to the table by pointing his open hand. The two deserters looked at each other and said, "We have a gun. Give us your food". Joseph pulled out a knife and held it in front of them and said, "I will take one of you down----that is for sure. My wife will clobber you both with her frying pan. Anna raised the frying pan and had a very serious expression on her face. The two deserters looked at each other and the taller one hesitated, but he put down his gun and said, "Yes, we are deserters, and we are hungry".

"Well, then, come and join us and we shall all be merry". The soldiers sat quietly at the table and Anna served them food. The taller one yawned and said, "We need a place to stay". Joseph hesitated, but then said, "Can you bring us food?" The taller one said, "Yes, I have a farmer friend who is three miles from here. He has planted rows and rows of fresh corn. We will leave in the morning for some fresh corn". Joseph said quietly, "Okay, then you can stay".

In the morning, the soldiers ate some soaked bread and cans of beans and drank some water, which came from the nearby stream. They left quietly, the taller one totting his gun. When they returned, they looked well-fed, but they still ate some of the corn that they had brought back.

Joseph and Anna watched them, and said nothing. When they had finished eating, they said, "By the way, you can have the rest". Joseph and Anna said, "Okay". There were a few cobs of fresh corn left for the Freier family. The soldiers continued to travel to the nearby farm and they gave Joseph and Anna the few pieces that remained. By the second month, the roar of cannons in the distance could be heard more and more times during the day and during the night.

The two deserters started to quarrel between themselves. They didn't know what to do. One wanted to visit the friend, the farmer and the other one wanted to stay inside and hide. They compromised. One stayed in. The other one went out, but he always took his rifle with him. When he was outside, he always looked over the terrain, and he always came back with stories that the farmer had told him about the armies moving closer nearby. By the third month of their visit with us, we knew that the war was really getting closer to us.

Joseph told Anna and the children, "We must leave here and soon. I just do not feel that it is safe any more. Anna agreed. Martin asked about the two soldiers, while one of them was sleeping, and Joseph said, "We will just leave him here".

They were to leave in two days. They needed the two days to plan where they were going and to plan for food and water. Most of all, they had to plan for water. Water was the key to survival and it always was in many ways. First of all, they followed the streams for directions; they were always able to find their way when they followed the streams; fish were abundant in the waters so they had a ready-made fresh food supply; bushes of berries and the smaller fruit trees like the quince trees needed the water nearby for their roots to absorb the water into their root systems.

Night came quickly these last two days, and it was a blessing. The cold weather was getting much colder. But their togetherness as a family helped them to overcome the chills from the coldness and the fears from the darkness and they were able to sleep soundly.

The deserter with the gun brought back corn most of the time, and just a few times some bread. It had gotten too dangerous for Josef's foreman to come to the woods to bring the usual drop of food so they appreciated whatever the deserter brought for them. This time the tall deserted brought a jug of home-made whiskey. The temptation and the lure of the taste of the whiskey drew the two deserters to drink to their heart's content on this night. The two deserters, they swooned back and forth. They crooned like coyotes.

Josef and Anna and their children were all huffing and puffing while this was going on. They prayed that no one nearby would hear the snoring or the soldier's sudden outbursts during their deep sleep. The sound reverberated so frequently. We were about to close our eyes, all of us out of sheer weakness, when the taller deserter started to snore even louder; his snoring had a sonata, a high-pitched rhythm all of its own; first a staccato beat and then two pangs on the drum, and the pang was not only high-pitched but it was lengthy.

On that particular night the sounds of the shooting from riflemen from the ground patrols, and the airplanes from high up above were coming closer to the woods where we were. We heard the sounds of the rotating wheels, grinding hard over the rocks and fallen trees and fallen buildings, from large tanks. The wheels of the tanks groaned just once in a while as they faltered, stalling just momentarily over the terrain, but then rejuvenated with a renewed power for destruction, just by the switch of the starter mechanism again. The Germans directed that their equipment and soldiers to: blast, and bombard, and destroy until they conquered and reached their destination.

Then the shouting, there were actual voices that were heard, we understood what they were saying; they were German soldiers and the officer in charge was giving his soldiers orders how to proceed against the Slovakian partisans who had joined Russian soldiers in the battle against the Germans, "Over here, shoot over here", he yelled out, and he yelled, "on the left of the hill". We heard cries for help in Slovakian, and in Russian, and in German. Anna and Josef understood all three languages. The two deserters continued to sleep through all of the noise.

Whenever we heard fast movements, fast footsteps, we were sure it was the Germans, and we dare not make a sound. From the tops of trees fires ignited as the smaller leaves caught fire. The fires spread from tree to tree as though passing from candlestick to candlestick, only a lot more serious. Branches charred and fell to the ground rapidly, igniting the ground beneath them and sometimes falling on an innocent soldier on the ground. The bodies of men who had died in the conflict burned too in the conflagration, turning the top of the ground into a bitter cold, hard, ground. Metals of destroyed tanks burned. The fumes and the piercing, acrid odors were impossible to escape. The deserters slept on. The moonshine was that effective. Anna and Josef and the children sat motionless in their chairs, expecting the worst. Josef told Anna, "If the snoring gets any louder, I will have to cover their mouths. I just do not know what else to do." Anna nodded her approval. Josef told her, "I will try to explain to them first what is happening and try to help them go into one of the back rooms. One thing is certain, if the soldiers are on the top of this bunker, and they are snoring, we have to do something!"

The battle continued. Running and running and shouting and shouting, and then stillness as some sharpshooters hid behind an embankment and shot, bullet after bullet, exhausting the rhythms of the guns. Slovaks could be heard for their voices were clear. The Slovaks were the ones who were the sharpshooters. They were close to our hidden bunker. Josef said to Anna, "If anyone could find us, it is the Slovaks. I wonder if that is good or bad."

Their thoughts were interrupted by the sudden sound of air craft flying overhead. The shocking sound of whistling bombs falling with their explosives to the ground could be heard—and we had to cover our ears or suffer from the reverberating echo. We prayed like never before that the bombs would stop. We prayed like never before that the war would finally stop.

I tried to think about the Bible. I tried to think about the battles between the Israelites and the early oppressors like Og, the Biblical character, who fought against the Israelites after they had just settled in the promised land. Battles were fierce and monumental---mostly hand-to-hand combat in those days, and there were: spear throwers and archers.

But the meaning behind the battle was the same as if I was riding the horse and had my sword drawn----riding faster and faster, and yet faster until I could see the eyes of the man who would either kill me or I would kill him. At least I would see the feelings of a soldier in his eyes. I could feel that his heart was in the right place and that he was defending a cause. There were no eyes of real soldiers to be seen in this war and there certainly were no righteously causes.

Our hearts beat doubly fast as we had a telescope to see what flag was hung above us. Then maybe we could breathe easier. We listened with our ears as our hearts pounded, following the sad, sad ballad of battle sounds. There was smoke, so much smoke---it filtered into our cave. But our real vision of thought was not obscured.

But the protagonists, the Nazis vision of thought was obscured long ago as the arch protagonists drew their warring strategic maps and plans across fields and plains of magnificent mountains and valleys like ours in our country, Czechoslovakia, and other monumental countries like England, France, Poland, just to name a few. Czechoslovakia would never be the same; this history was indelible in fact and in our minds. What about its people? Will they survive? Will they have freedom? Will we as Jews have the freedom to pray our prayers as we had done for two millenniums, two thousand years of our prayers that is what it amounts to----reaching out to do what the angels will approve of. I want to cry out, "Stop the Nazis." Stop them now. Kill them before they kill us." We want another 2,000 years of prayers to our G-d. We want another 2,000 years of heritage and devotion to our God. My head shakes back and forth, back and forth from the pressure of when this will all stop.

There is a unity of thought amongst us: a singing of souls and sad songs; there is a unity of commission for our people: we want our people to survive and we want to be part of a thriving Jewish community once again. There is our unity of hope and that is undying. We dare not stand up, at this moment to express our thoughts. We might be heard. Life, causes, values all seem value less. To the victor belong the vanquished. If the Germans win, how many of the German people will enjoy the spoils of the war? Very few will enjoy any of the spoils. Only the despots will reap the harvest from the pools of blood from the innocent and the unaware. A life has no value these war-torn days and life will be meaningless in days to follow also.

When there are no prayers and the laws and commandments of God to follow, there is no reverence for life. G-d did not allow Abraham to slay his son, Issac for the most important reason: he wanted a reverence for life and for the living; he wanted a song for the living; he wanted a Ten Commandments for the living to follow. What will there be of the worship to G-d then.

I think that we as Jews will never allow ourselves to lose our G-d. I think that we will live through this battle, and whatever battles come. Others who will die for our cause, which is basically the cause for freedom are angels who are put here on earth; who are the soldiers of God's armada, and who will ultimately in time defeat the Nazi devils, and destroy them completely; and when they feel they have accomplished their goal and reinforced the warmth of their heartfelt endeavors for another set of generations and generations; they will then relay a report to the master himself and request permission for time off for a job well-done for they have done well at God's instructions and bidding.

Josef poked the taller deserter gently with a twig at the top of his shoulder every time he began to snore; and instinctively, the tall deserter would gently push Josef's hand away. We began to hear more and more footsteps coming closer and closer; then running, running closer and closer-------it was at first hard to determine if they were in the front or the middle or the back of the bunker. One thing was certain, the war had come to us—there were soldiers who were running, then shouting, then rifles were shooting; then we heard the sound of grenades popping. The very strong pine boulders and the beech tree wood inserts which were constructed in a fashion to build a solid underground bunker held fast, except for an occasional minor crack in the ceiling.

Joseph motioned for Anna to sit next to the shorter deserter and he sat next to the taller deserter; the children fell asleep where they were sitting, all covered in blankets. The cannons roared like lions, who had been deprived of food for a day and were on the prowl and were going to eat at whatever the cost; all night the bombs fell.

Human voices, shouts of pain, unconscionable woe from seeping wounds, could be heard throughout the night-----absolutely the worst

opera to listen to. It was at least a day and one-half later before the noise of
the opera music of this sadistic war ended. And when the silence began, the
music of hopeful defeat of the oppressor began and we opened our eyes; it
was hard to believe that the conflict had stopped; the silence was for a few
minutes a deafening sound, but only for a few moments. My father and
mother were now able to sleep for a few hours and Sam and I took over
watching the two deserters. We took over the same roles and hoped that
we could control their snoring. As more and more of the hours passed, and
more and more days went by, we began to hear the natural sounds of the
forest: the sound of the wolf, the sound of the woodpecker, the hooting
sound of the owl, and there could have been no greater, or more talented
sounds than these sounds; they were my symphony of music, the finest
symphony in the world. Now five had passed and all is quite and my father
and I will go outside for some food. We will be cautious. We will need
some food. We will take the fishing pole and go to the stream. We are all
hankering for some a good fish dinner---it could be raw—we like it wet
and raw, eaten with fresh wild mushroom and wild onions.

At the prompting of the shorter deserter, Joseph said it was all right
to open up the hatch of the bunker. The three men, the smaller deserter,
Josef, and Martin emerged from the hidden bowels of the earth and
carefully closed the hatch to their survivor unit. Smoke with the odors of
burnt woods, gun powder residue filters flew through the air, the ground
was heated with singeing small fires here and there; bodies of men who
once lived lay in forever stillness on the blackened ashes of the earth; their
words and thoughts for peace would never be known. Better they should
have toiled in hardship all the days of their lives and to have held their
heads in righteous affirmation. Bless God for his thoughts of peace and
for his blessings.

Joseph stumbled and blew on his handkerchief, and said to Martin,
"Go tell your mother that we are leaving this place now. "Pick up whatever
you can. We must leave this hideout. We must leave now. It is no longer
safe to be here. They will be back to bury their dead. And they will fight
again here. The war is not over yet. There are safer places higher up in the
mountains----let us just follow the streams".

There was no discussion about what was going on. Everyone knew
that they must follow what Joseph said. With heads bowed down, and
expressionless faces, and with eyes half-closed, and sadness in their
hearts, they each packed whatever food there was and rolled it in their
knapsacks.

Very little time passed when Joseph demanded, "let us go!" and they all followed behind him. One by one they emerged from the opening in the earth, as though the dead had risen from their coffins, but not quite. They had not died. They had faced life in many of the toughest situations possible.

When they were all standing firmly on the outside, Martin mentioned to Joseph in a soft tone of voice, "Pop, I remembered to take the Bible". Instinctively Joseph nodded his head in affirmation, "Good, you did the right thing. I am proud of you. We certainly do not want the Germans to find it".

They knelt down for silent prayer, and Joseph quickly pointed to some black, bark colored trees, which were standing straight, as though they were guards for the innocent fleeing people; most of the branches of the trees seem to point their branches towards the west-----Josef told his family, "We must follow the natural signs and the streams; let us go five yards to the left and head west and then follow the stream all the west; I will tell everyone when to stop; and they headed deep into nascent, pristine, peaceful country; a family of five men and two women blended into the forest, as though they were shadows of trees moving with the wind toward their destination: a life of wholeness and fulfillment and peace.

Fallen leaves rustled with the wind and crackled from the weight of their footsteps. Owls peered at them with rotating corneas from high up in the branches of the trees. Squirrels paused from their staccato paces and with arched-up hind legs, paused to look at them with their large bleating, black rotating eyes; rabbits paused to shake their forward leaning ears to hear our footsteps, as they continued on their trek for some tasty, choice, green foliage. Mice scampered at a faster pace under the rustling leaves, nervously running towards a camouflaged hole, which was well hidden by underbrush. Chipmunks stopped to peer at them with anxious rotating dark black eyes; as they waved their little furry tails, but dodged quickly over a rotted fallen tree and scurried along to their hideout hole.

The seven of them forged on, further and further, deeper and deeper into the woods: forgetting hunger; forgetting thirst; but remembering that dawn turns into dusk; and that hope and prayers light up the heavens. After half of a day of walking through the pristine unknown area of the woods, Josef whispered a breath, "look over there". The eyes of each one was following the pathway of his pointing right finger. They saw an opening in a natural cave that looked like it was easy to get to.

Joseph breathed in and out easier, as he said in a soft-tone of voice, "this will be our new home", and they all followed him, even if they had to drag their legs, into the entrance of the cave. Sam was the last to go in. Martin held him by his hand and nudged him to come in.

The cave was darker than the first cave, alluding to the idea that there were no natural openings. They lay down their shattered belongings and their weary selves. They lay down on the cold damp floor, oblivious to outside world's cruelties and in deep sleep.

Emerging from their hibernation very slowly the next morning, as the light opened up the day and filtered through the opening of the cave. Instinctively, they opened up their knapsacks and munched on kernels of raw corn, and sour berries, and dried-out morsels of bread. They shared one jug of water. Sam did not speak at first but started to speak about how beautiful the trees were around the cave a little bit later. Martin coughed at times, but when Josef asked who was willing to go with him to the woods to catch some fish, there was a quick response from Martin and from Sam. They both responded simultaneously "yes", and they walked out of the cave proudly with Josef with their thoughts focused on catching the grayling and enjoying eating it for supper.

ABOUT THE AUTHOR

Cheryl Freier can hop on the train and be in Boston in 20 minutes. It is the culture of the Boston City that has inspired her to maintain optimum literacy and to become a published author. She has been a preschool teacher. She has two grown daughters.